I never did picture any boy I knew
sitting beside me . . .

It was always a man I had seen, in the Sears catalog. He was wearing a gray suit. He was tall and straight like the boards Pa used to add another room on our house and he had blue eyes, the color of the ice in winter on the Nemaha River behind our house in Salem. Not the translucent blue-green of robins' eggs, but a liquidy blue that got darker the closer you looked. Just like the Nemaha through the ice. His hair would be parted on the right and one big wave would go up toward the back of his head. It would be real light—almost blonde—the tan color of the mushrooms that Ma said were good for eating. He'd turn toward me and I'd smile, ever so slightly, and—

The yellow canaries were singing as I swung in the hammock. The grass waved slightly; watching it, I almost felt hypnotized. Maybe that was why I didn't hear anybody coming.

I looked up into his face; then jumped up and gasped.

"I didn't mean to scare you," he said.

"You didn't." That was the truth. It wasn't the suddenness of his approach that scared me. It was his appearance—he *was* the man in the Sears catalog, the man I had dreamed about; the very man with blue eyes like the Nemaha River. His light-blond hair, just like in my visions, was parted on the right and one big wave went up toward the back of his head.

I must have looked shocked, for he continued, "My name's Porter—Porter Baker. I came up with the Hessers."

I was glad to walk in the house and be with the others. I needed time to think, to look at him from a distance, to pinch myself to make sure I was awake.

INA

Karen Baker Kletzing

Serenade/Saga
B O O K S
of the Zondervan Publishing House
Grand Rapids, Michigan

F
K

INA
Serenade/Saga is an imprint of Zondervan Publishing House, 1415 Lake Drive, SE, Grand Rapids, Michigan, 49506.

ISBN 0-310-46402-1

Edited by Anne Severance and Janet Wilson
Designed by Kim Koning
Printed in the United States of America

84 85 86 87 88 89 / 10 9 8 7 6 5 4 3 2 1

To my grandma, Ina, whose wonderful memory for detail made it possible for me to write her story. May her life inspire others as it has mine.

CHAPTER 1

Summer, 1886

IT WASN'T UNTIL LATER THAT I found out what my name really meant. Ma had told me that Grandpa named me Ina after a character in a book he had been reading. I heard the "naming story" so many times that soon I knew every word of it by heart.

"Why, she sure is pretty. Let me name her Ina," he had said.

"O.K., Pa, but don't get any ideas about spoiling her like the Ina in the book you told me about."

"What you worried about, Clara? You weren't spoiled, were ya?"

When I was little I'd always ask, "What does *spoiled* mean, Ma?"

"Well, Ina," she would explain, "you know sometimes if we don't get our ham smoked soon enough, it spoils."

I'd hold my nose, remembering the awful smell.

"And then it's no good to anyone," Ma would continue, "makes you sick to be around—could kill ya if you eat it."

"Well, I sure don't wanna be like that ham."

"You won't, Ina. I'll whip ya every day to make sure!"

I'd say, "No, Ma!" and go screaming out of the house, holding my bottom, hearing Ma's laugh. It was a game we played.

Ma always said I was the prettiest of the four girls. I think she'd say that because I had brown hair the same color as hers.

"It's the color of molasses." Ma would whisper the next part because you never knew when Pa would show up. "Charlie Richards used to say to me, 'Clara, a man could get stuck real good in that sweet molasses hair of yours.'"

When we lived in Oklahoma, I'd sneak a comb out in my corset, climb up in the wild cherry tree, and brush my hair for hours. But I always told Ma I was going out to watch the yellow canaries.

"She sure is crazy about those yellow birds, Pa."

"Well, at least she keeps the birds away from the cherries."

Pa would ruffle my hair when I came in and ask, "How's my pretty little scarecrow today? Did you flap your arms like this?" and he'd pretend to fly off out the door.

In the cherry tree I'd hold one strand of hair and swivel my body on the branch till the sunlight hit it just right. *When somebody courts me*, I thought, *it's got to be outside with my back toward the west so they can see the sun come streaking through my hair.* I always talked silently to myself except when a canary would land real close and cock his head my way. Then I'd raise my voice, "Right over there." I'd point my comb at the hammock down by the black walnut tree, and the canary would nod his head.

The truth is I don't think I was scaring any birds out of that tree because I'd quit brushing and sit trance-like, my eyes on the swing. I never did picture any boy I knew sitting there beside me. It was always a man I had seen, in the Sears catalog. He was wearing a gray suit. He was tall and straight like the boards Pa used to add another room on our house and he had blue eyes, the color of the ice in winter on the Nemaha River behind our house in Salem. Not the translucent blue-green of robins' eggs, but a liquidy blue that got darker the closer you looked. Just like the Nemaha through the ice. You never could see the bottom. But if you leaned down with your nose almost touching the surface, you could see inside the river. (Pa always said it wasn't the inside of the river you could see—it was the river's heart.)

His hair, like the man's in the catalog, would be parted on the right and one big wave would go up toward the back of his head. It would be real light—almost blond—the tan color of the mushrooms that Ma said were good for eating. He'd turn toward me and stare at the golden glow the sun made around my hair. I'd smile, ever so slightly, and he'd recite the little poem that Grandpa Wilson had sent to Grandma in one of his letters,

How sweet at close of silent eve
The harp's responsive sound;
How sweet the vows that ne'er deceive,
And deeds by virtue crown'd!
How sweet to sit beneath a tree
In some delightful grove;
But oh! more soft, more sweet to me,
The voice of her I love.

And then I'd say another line I had read in one of
Ma's letters to Pa when they were engaged, "My pen
is poor; my ink is pale; my love for you can never
fail." It never crossed my mind that this line didn't
make much sense, as I said it instead of wrote it. Since
these were the only lines of love poetry I had ever
read, I thought they fit in fine.

But I wouldn't let him touch my hair even though
he was dying to and his fingers trembled ever so close
to it. I'd just shake my head, pretending I hadn't seen
his fingers sneaking up and say, "Oh, that's so lovely. Do tell me more."

Ma had said, "Looking is before marriage; touching is after. Why, look at those apples sitting on the
table over there. You know how often I have to slap
little Martin's hand when he reaches out for another,
with one already clenched between his teeth, juice
dripping all over? Yep, what you touch, you gotta
take. And what you take, you gotta eat. That's why I
always say. . ." By now my sisters, Lulu and Elsie,
and I would join Ma in a chorus: "Looking is before
marriage; touching is after."

But love poetry and touching weren't the real reasons I dreamed about courting and marriage. It was because I didn't want to be alone in the dark. The first time Ma caught me with the light on, she said I might catch the house afire and how would I feel then? Well, that scared me enough not to try it again for a few nights. But soon the nightmare would get the best of me and seemed worse than my fear of catching the house afire. The next time I turned it on Pa came to talk to me. He spoke real quiet—not like Ma—explaining the cost of kerosene and how leaving a light on all night cost more than a whole week of after-dinner light. Knowing how much Pa liked to read made me sad to waste kerosene. I almost told him why I wanted the light on when he hugged me, but I thought he might laugh at me or tell Ma. So I just cried in my pillow after he blew out the flame.

Many nights I'd recite the Twenty-third Psalm, the one we had to memorize in school. When I got to, "Yea, though I walk through the valley of the shadow of death, I will fear no evil," I'd say it over and over. I wasn't quite sure what it meant, except I knew what shadows were from my nightmare. And I knew little Cousin Lottie couldn't see in that black box they put her in even though Ma said she really wasn't there. But I saw her. I knew she was there.

"There would have been two deaths in the family except for the mercy of the Good Man," Ma would say, pointing toward the sky. "You both had diphtheria, you know."

Well, I couldn't pronounce the sickness, but I remember trying to swallow and feeling a lump so big I couldn't eat, till Grandpa Martin pulled out what looked like a long, stringy wad of cotton.

So that's it, I thought. *I swallowed some of Ma's cotton.*

The nice part of diphtheria was never being alone. I'd lie awake so the nightmare wouldn't come, wishing I'd get diphtheria again.

I couldn't have been more than three at the time, since it happened in Kansas and we moved to Nebraska before Lulu was born. I bet Ma thought I'd forgotten it, but I never did. Annabel and I had been looking for a place to be alone to tell secrets. Since we had to whisper, it had to be a nice, quiet place. We found an empty room where Ma kept her sewing and extra blankets. I propped Annabel up against the wall and then knelt down next to her, so I could hear her when she whispered. I was just in the middle of a good giggle spell (the corn kernels on Annabel kept tickling my chin), when baby Elsie started crying.

Annabel suggested I shut the door so we could continue secret-telling. Pretty soon Annabel said she'd like a piece of Ma's apple pie and I agreed, so we went to open the door. But it wouldn't open! It was like somebody was pulling on the knob from the other side, keeping it closed. I started yelling, "Ma! Pa! Carl!" as loud as I could. I hit the door till the sides of my palms turned red. Then I remembered that this room was at the end of a long hall, and I knew they couldn't hear me. I thought about jumping out the window, but I was up so high I knew I might break my neck. Then I sat down in the corner to cry with Annabel. When we woke up, the moon had made shadows across the walls. They seemed to move as if they were alive. I thought they were the animals Pa shot and killed—only giant-size—come back to haunt. A squirrel, a bird with teeth as long as my arm and ready to pounce. As it grew darker the animals left and I clung to Annabel. Then the door opened and a light said, "Ina, you in there?" and Ma's arms were around me.

"Oh, Ma! I don't ever want to be alone in the dark again!"

I think that is why I was so good in school. The first day the teacher put George Miller in the closet when a paper wad landed in her hair comb. When George got out, he said, "Aw, I weren't scared atall—just killed me a dozen rats or so." Everybody laughed at this. George always exaggerated. Everybody laughed except me, that is. I didn't want to go back the next day, but Pa made me. So I didn't speak much but kept a book in front of me all the time. I raced Carl home from school every day, so I could practice my running. If the teacher ever tried to put me in the closet, I'd run on home so fast she'd never catch me. I always took the seat next to the door for that reason.

I could barely read when the Bible contest was announced, but I knew I wanted that Bible more than anything in the world! Before he would read the Bible at the table, Pa always quoted the verse: "Thy word is a lamp unto my feet and a light unto my path." I figured if I could have a Bible in my room at night, it would never be dark in there. I sure didn't know how it worked, though. When everyone would leave the table, I'd examine that Book real good, but I couldn't ever find any kerosene in it, or even a wick. I only knew if Pa said it was so, it was so.

I had to memorize a verse for every letter in the alphabet. Ma said twenty-six verses were too many for a little girl like me and it would only "frustrate" me. I didn't know what that meant, but Pa kept saying, "Let her try, Clara. Let her try."

So I tried to learn a verse every night, with time out for Saturday and a review on Sunday. I figured that would take me a little over five weeks. The contest was six weeks away, so I had some time to review. Pa would put aside his book to help me. I reckon he learned them, too. I liked the *C* verse best of all because it was so short: "Children, obey your parents." The *F* verse took a long time to learn, but if I took a deep breath and said it real fast, I could say the whole verse without missing a word. "For-God-so-loved-the-world-that-He-gave-His-only-begotten-son-that-whosoever-believeth-in-Him-should-not-perish-but-have-everlasting-life."

Pa spent a long time explaining *begotten* while I impatiently twirled my braid around my finger. "Pa, why can't they just say, God *made* Him instead of *begot* Him? And why can't it say *die* instead of *perish*?"

"Because that's the way it is, Ina." When Pa got upset or nervous he stroked his beard real fast. He was doing it now.

And on the day of the contest, Pa was stroking his beard extra fast. He and Ma sat up in the front row.

Carl said he was gonna make me laugh, and I said, "Well, I just won't look at ya."

"Oh, I'm so handsome, you can't help it!"

It took me twice as long to lace my shoes that day. Ma had made me a new white dress and I was so proud of it. But the best part was seeing that Bible sitting on the stand by the teacher, Nanny Allen. If I won tonight, there would be no more nightmares. I'd just open up the Bible, set it on the chair by my bed, and have light the whole night. Ma and Pa couldn't say no, because I had won it and it was mine.

When I started out reciting my verses, I was watching Pa and Ma. But Pa was saying all the verses with his mouth. I thought maybe I'd be accused of cheating if I kept watching him, so I quit. When I got to the *F* verse, I couldn't think of that long word Pa had explained to me. I knew it started with a *b*. I looked all around. It was too early to lose. Two girls had already sat down. It was just starting to come into my head when Pa blurted out, "Begotten."

"Mr. Wilson!" Nanny Allen said. She was trying to say something else, but she couldn't be heard above the laughing. Pa was all red and kept taking out his hanky and wiping the back of his neck.

Pa would just feel terrible if he ruined it for me, so I stepped over to Miss Allen and whispered, "I had just thought of it myself when Pa said it."

I think Miss Allen was relieved not to make me sit down, too. Everyone cheered when I continued. Ma said I was the favorite because I was the youngest. I was getting tired of standing even though we had practiced on a box at home. I would have been O.K. if

15

Freddie had not gotten to say his *O* verse over and over. It was because of his lisp that Miss Allen let him. Freddie also had buck teeth, polished to almost a shine. His teeth rose rhythmically up and down, up and down, as he spoke. I guess this was kinda hypnotizing me (that's what Ma said later when I told her about it), because I started to sway back and forth and close my eyes. It was Carl who saved me—Carl and one of his dumb ol' tricks.

I guess in all the excitement of getting everybody ready, Ma had forgotten to check Carl's pockets, or else Carl had hidden one in his mouth. An acorn lid is really so small you could hide it anywhere. Judging from the blissful look on Carl's face after he had sneaked it up to his mouth and given the loudest acorn whistle I had ever heard, he must have been just itching all through the contest to do it. Pa immediately grabbed it out of his mouth and, all over the room, I saw "pocket checks" being made on Carl's friends. Sure enough, you could hear the acorn tops dropping on the floor in the silence that followed. So Carl was going to have a band!

Well, it woke me up and the rest of the contest went as smooth as buttermilk. Even so, it was like a dream come true to hear my name called. Nanny Allen said to her recollection I was the youngest who ever had won a Bible contest. Pa looked like he did when he heard Lulu was born.

Afterwards we had fancy cookies—the kind you order at Christmas from the Sears catalog, with the pink frosting—and lemonade. All the rest of the afternoon, Ma would drag me from person to person and

16

thrust me forward, saying, "Ain't she a whiz? Got her Ma's brains, I guess." After we left each person, she'd spit on her hand and redo one of my curls that kept coming undone and tie the bow on the back of my dress. All I wanted to do was get home. I held the Bible tight in my hands.

The buggy ride home was the longest I'd ever taken. When I finally got alone in my room, I undressed slowly and carefully laid out my dress. It was like the night before Christmas. I wanted to make the expectation last as long as possible. I blew out the lamp but, tonight, I wasn't afraid of the dark. I leaned over to open the Bible lying on the chair next to my bed. I lay back quickly on my bed, expecting to be blinded by a bright splash of light. But nothing happened. I turned to a different page in the Bible. The room was just as dark as before. I took the Bible on my lap, licking my fingers so I could turn each page. After the last page, I turned my face toward the pillow.

Why did God let me think such things were true? Maybe I just wasn't good enough for it to work. Since Annabel always had the same nightmare I did, I wasn't sure which one of us woke up screaming.

CHAPTER 2

Spring, 1895

THERE WERE OTHER CONTESTS IN SCHOOL with less disappointing outcomes than the Bible contest. Every year in the spring the school had a children's day exercise. Elsie and I always got new dresses and slippers—brown ones with only one tie, not like the high-topped black shoes we wore in the winter. But this year was special. We had signed up to be on the program. Ma made us matching dresses out of calico and percale—red ones with white horseshoes on them and, best of all, lace. When I was wearing that dress, it didn't even bother me to see Priscilla Newsbickle in her white slippers. She was always looking at them just so others would. She knew she was the only one in school whose Pa could afford to buy 'em.

Ma taught us a song she had learned when she was

little—"Two Little Maids"—and we made up the motions to go with it.

Two Little Maids

Once there lived side by side,
Two little maids.
Used to dress just alike,
Hair down in braids,
Blue gingham pinafores, stockings of red,
Little sunbonnets tied on each head.
School days are over, secrets they tell
Whispering arm in arm down by the well.
One day a quarrel came, how tears were shed
"You can't play in my yard."
And the other said:

Chorus:

"I don't want to play in your yard.
I don't like you any more.
You'll be sorry when you see me sliding
  down our cellar door.
You can't holler down our rain-barrel;
You can't climb our apple tree.
I don't want to play in your yard,
If you won't be good to me."

Next day two little maids, each other missed.
Quarrels were soon made up, sealed with a kiss.
They're hand in hand again, happy they go,
Friends all through life to be.
They love each other so. (We repeated the chorus here)

School days have passed away—
Sorrow and bliss.
But love that remembers, yet quarrel and kiss,

I've sweet dreams of childhood.
We hear the cry:
"You can't play in my yard"
And the old reply: (Now we did the chorus again.)

Sometimes Elsie would get to giggling so much that you couldn't understand the words. This was all right with me except during the part where we were supposed to cry and say, "Boo-hoo, boo-hoo."

Everyone liked it so much at the children's day exercise that we got to perform at another children's contest. Pa would say we got our "theatrical talent" from him but Ma would say, "Now, Pa, it's from my side of the family. Why, didn't my brothers win a medal at the State Fair?"

I did like to sing—especially in church. I'd listen for the sound of my voice and think maybe I could be like that Jenny Lind and travel around and become rich and famous. The first thing I'd buy would be white slippers, maybe two pairs. Then I'd come back into town in a brand-new buggy, with red velvet seats and trim to match, and drive by Priscilla Newsbickle's white house.

Singing always set me to dreaming, so I never did listen much in church except when Maudie Picketts and Sadie Fields prayed. They'd get so excited and loud even ol' Grandpa Hasket would quit snoring and look around. I didn't know how they could get so excited about praying. Ma and Pa were quiet pray-ers and, if I ever decided to pray again, I knew I would be, too.

Because I wanted to be a famous singer some day and travel the world, geography was my favorite subject. I just loved running my fingers over those raised bumps that represented mountains on the maps and saying the names: *Himalayas, Tauras, Caucasus*. And sometimes I'd sneak in from recess just to trace the blue snaky lines of rivers. My favorite was the Amazon because it was so long.

Usually Nanny Allen left me to dream in silence but one day she said, "Ina, we just got a new world map yesterday. Would you like to take that old one home?" I took my finger off the Virgin Islands and looked at her. "Here's a box for the tacks and a string to tie around the map when you get it rolled up."

I was so excited. I held the map in my lap the rest of the day. I was going to try and sneak off without Carl and Elsie just to be alone with my thoughts.

Looking down from the hill the school was on, I could see as far as the depot and our two-story brick house behind it. The trees with their yellow and red snow apples looked as small as leafy carrot tops in our garden. The flour mill wheel looked like one of Dad's black shirt buttons. The flame from McCool's Blacksmith Shop was a tiny flicker. *Just imagine how small things must look from the top of Kilimanjaro*, I thought. *How I would like to see that!*

"Hey, what you got, Ina?" Carl's voice broke into my thoughts. When Carl found out what it was, he teased me the whole mile-and-a-half walk home from school, with Elsie giggling at everything he said. "What do you want with that, Ina? You'll never get out of Salem, Nebraska. You ain't got 'traveling blood' in ya. You got 'stay-at-home blood,' and ya can't change that."

Elsie giggled but I just kept on walking faster. I'd show Carl what kind of blood I had. He'd see.

After Carl's teasing I kept my dreams to myself except for sharing them with Jesse—and Clare. Jesse bought old railroad irons for scrap and sold them. He lived across the tracks from us next to the depot. I'd watch the trains come in and go out while Jesse would talk about the longest train ride he had ever taken (from New York to Iowa) and about all the places he'd seen. He'd end every story by saying, "But I never did cross an ocean, no, sir. Sure would have liked to have done that." When I unrolled my map for him, he just whistled.

"Look at all that water, Jesse."

"Cross it for me, Ina," Jesse said, putting his hand on my shoulder. "Cross it for me."

Clare was my best friend. After I met Clare, Annabel and I never told secrets anymore. Clare and I always made sure we were on the same team when we played baseball, and we found each other the smoothest stones for hopscotch. Clare drew the straightest lines for four-square I ever saw. The squares were so even that Priscilla wanted to play with us, but she had to bring her own block to kick over the lines.

But there was one boy that never played four-square with us. He never played with anyone. His milky blue eyes and pink strawberry skin made Clare and me think he should have been a girl, except for his big lips. They kind of rolled as he talked and seemed to get in the way of his tongue. Because of this, they were always wet and looked like a baby's lips when he drooled. Everett's hair never seemed combed. A big

22

blond chunk of it hung over his eyes like it was ready to fall out any minute.

But Everett always tried. When he tried to tie his shoes, the teacher had to get scissors to cut out the knot. The rest of the year his shoes kept coming off on the playground. He tried to play ball, but the ball would always go right between his legs. His hands were too slippery to walk across the chin-up bar. The swing broke when he sat down. Since it was that cloth kind, it couldn't be fixed. Every recess it hung there, lifeless, its broken strands moving slightly in the wind. We'd all remember what happened and laugh. After that, Everett just leaned against the corner of the fence when we went out for recess, rubbing the rough edges of the wood.

The teacher must have noticed Everett just standing and watching, leaning against the wooden fence, because she asked him if he would bring in wood for the stove. Now this put Todd out a bit since it had always been the duty of the oldest boy in the school.

"Why, it's tradition," Todd said, "and look at Everett—he can't even carry an armload without dropping half of it."

Part of the problem was that Everett was fat and not as strong as Todd. After this, when it was Everett's turn to read, Todd always laughed, and mocked him after school.

"Listen!" Todd would shout standing on a stump, holding a book in his hands. "Hear Everett read: 'The—ah—er—er—h-h-hats were bl-bl-black and I—I—I am f—f—fat.'

Todd traded desks so Everett had to pass him every

time he went to the blackboard. This meant at least two attempted trippings a day. He managed to time them when Miss Allen's back was turned.

She'd wheel around and ask, "Everett, who tripped you?"

"Why, no one, ma'am," Everett would reply.

To make it worse, Everett was poor—the poorest boy in school. The fifty-pound flour sacks we made dishtowels out of, Everett wore for shirts. While Carl, Elsie, and I had ham or beef sandwiches for lunch, Everett's were lard. When the Chatauqua would come to town, Everett never had a ticket to see the dancers or hear the singers. Since the fairground was right next to our house, Pa bought him a ticket once to go to the fair, but Everett said no. I think he was just too embarrassed about his clothes.

I thought Everett was through trying, but I was wrong. Maybe he wouldn't have tried except for the tornado. The sky had started to darken. Clare and I quit swinging and ran into the school building, holding hands. Even Everett looked up from the corner of the fence and turned to walk slowly in. One of the boys threw down his bat, shouting, "Tornado!" The smallest girl in our class began to cry.

I huddled under the table in the darkness next to Clare. I felt hot. A face was moving towards me. Everett's mouth closed and puckered. Our lips, when they touched, made a slippery sound like Ma's wet mop on the floor. My chin began to drip. Everett was staring. His eyes weren't milky anymore, but blue like the colored crystal in a cat's-eye marble and they glistened. He wasn't looking at my curls, but straight into my eyes. He seemed to be trying to see something inside me; I didn't know what. Everett wiped his eyes on his flour-sack shirt. I thought I was going to be sick.

It was a week before I told Clare about it. I never did tell Ma or anyone else, but always walked fast past the corner of the woodpile where Everett was, my hand in Clare's, my eyes on the ground.

When school broke for the summer, I forgot about Everett until one rainy July night. Ma came home from one of her nursing cases and was real quiet—not like Ma at all.

"This probably means somebody died," Carl whispered to me.

"Hush, Carl. Ma will speak when she's ready to."

Ma wasn't ready to until the next morning. After breakfast she called Carl and me over to the corner where she was rocking all by herself. "I know you two would wanna know this because you went to school with him. Everett Koop died last night. He had the whooping cough. If he had been thinner, we might have been able to save him. But he just had a harder time breathing than most. I talked to him and told him my children would pray for him, but he just couldn't hang on."

I broke away from Ma's hand and ran out and hid behind the woodpile to think. I felt somehow responsible for Everett's death. Maybe whooping cough wasn't what he died from—maybe Ma made that up. Maybe he died from being left alone. And now I wouldn't get a second chance. It seemed like God had tricked me again—letting Everett die before I could help him.

They had the funeral at the schoolhouse, but I didn't go. It was bad enough just thinking about the day he kissed me, but to think those thick pink lips were all white and cold made me shake all over. Clare told me Todd came all dressed up and weeping like he'd lost his own mother. Well, maybe that's how he eased his conscience. As for me, I was not gonna weep over what was gone, but would try to make it up to Everett by waiting for a chance to help somebody else.

My chance came sooner than I expected. Grandpa Martin wrote that Grandma Melissee was feeling sickly and could I help out by taking care of Lilly? Ma said, "Well, I don't know. . . you've been a big help with the new baby." Martin had been born in May.

"Ah, Ma, let me go." I guess maybe Ma must have known somehow how important it was to me, because she finally said yes.

The night before I was to leave, I dreamed Everett was in the closet. I was outside the door trying to pry it open and get him out. He was screaming, "Ina, help me!" but I couldn't. I ran to look for someone else but no one was there. When I woke up I was holding a piece of the wooden bedpost that Pa had been promising Ma he would nail back on. The only thing I could think about was, "Who's gonna carry in the wood for Miss Allen next year? Todd's graduated and I can't get Everett out of the closet."

CHAPTER 3

Summer, 1896

I WAS SO GLAD TO BE getting away from home and the schoolhouse which carried so many memories of Everett, that I wasn't even afraid of what Lilly would be like. But I was eager to see Grandpa and Grandma.

Ma always said Grandpa was partial to me, I just couldn't wait to see what candy he had waiting just for me in their little cupboard. And Grandma Melissee was so sweet. I packed the silver dress she had made me two years ago, even though it was too short and tight around the neck now.

I knew Grandpa would tell me stories every night and read, "Little Red Riding Hood." The rolls of his tummy shook so much when he laughed that I could feel them bounce off my back when I was sitting on his lap. And his moustache, always stiff with beeswax, would have the faint smell of "Doctor's Choice" tobacco from his pipe.

The only time I'd seen him sad was when he was talking about Lilly or one of the cases he'd doctored and lost.

When Grandpa's buggy drove up, it smelled like the pharmacy corner of the general store back home. "Here, Ina, you drive for a while," he said, handing me the reins.

"Pa would never let me drive the buggy back home," I said, somewhat in awe.

"Well, now, we're not back home, are we?"

Grandma Melissee wore little curls that shook when she talked and shook more when she laughed. When I visited she always took out her shells for me to look at. She was from California, and I guess they reminded her of home.

As we sat down to eat, Grandpa said, "Well, we can eat our dinner in peace since Lilly is sleeping."

"Yes, thank the Lord," Grandma sighed.

Ma said it rode heavy on Grandpa that he, being a doctor, couldn't even help his own daughter. After dinner he pushed his plate away and said he had to check on a couple of new babies who had been acting poorly. Grandma Melissee said she'd take me in to see Lilly so we could get acquainted.

Lilly was lying on her bed, her face toward the wall. She was such a peculiar gray color that I thought she must be dead. When we got closer, I could see that her skin was mottled—white and light brown and black, like Ma's sausages. Ma said she was fifteen but she looked eighty to me.

"This is Ina—she's gonna stay with us for a while." Lilly turned her head slowly. Her eyes were that same milky blue color as Everett's, only paler.

"Hello, Lilly."

"Lilly doesn't speak much," said Grandma Melissee. "Let's let a little light in here before the sun sets. Ina, get that book over there and read to Lilly. Her favorite story is about Jesus' raising Lazarus."

So I read while Lilly just stared. I don't know what she was looking at or if she even listened. When I finished the story of Lazarus, I read about Jesus—changing water into wine, healing the blind man, choosing His disciples. It was getting hard to see, and I was feeling lonely when Grandma Melissee came in with some of the soup we had had for supper.

"Now didn't you like that, Lilly?" Lilly didn't move. Grandma held her up while I spooned soup into her mouth. It reminded me of the time I had watched a robin feed her babies—they just held their mouths open, and she dropped the worms in. After every bite Lilly took, some soup dribbled out, and I'd wipe it away with a towel. When the soup was gone, Grandma said, "There, Lilly, maybe tomorrow you'll feel like walking outside and sitting on the porch."

I went to bed disappointed. I thought nursing and helping people would bring satisfaction, 'cause of course they'd thank you and hold your hand. I bet Everett would have. Lilly probably didn't even know I was there. I felt kinda cheated again Oh, well, at least I got to sleep in the main room which wasn't dark but lighted all night. Grandpa kept Lilly's door open so he could hear her, and the light was on all night.

Grandpa was already gone when I got up. Lilly and I sat on the porch, and I read the story of Lazarus to her again. When I finished, she said, "Mary, tell me more. You were there."

Grandma came out wiping her hands on her apron. "She thinks you're Lazarus' sister Mary." So that's who I was the rest of my visit. At first it was hard to answer to a different name but I got used to it.

Lilly mostly wanted to hear about Jesus. I described Him over and over from the picture that I remembered hanging on the school walls. I even quoted some of the verses from the Bible contest to make my stories more authentic. I wondered if Ma would say I was "sacriligious." She said that if ever anybody made up things about the "Good Man." I decided then that maybe God did serve a purpose. Maybe people like Lilly needed Him, but I didn't. Then there was the problem of Ma and Pa believing in Him, too. When I thought about this, I felt a little bit wiser and smarter—like I'd discovered something they hadn't.

One afternoon when I was just at the part where I was begging Jesus to come to Lazarus' tomb, Lilly tugged at my sleeve and lifted one bony finger to her lips. She whispered, "Now don't tell anyone, but I'm not really Lilly. I'm Lazarus." Lilly sat back and smiled, content that her secret was safe with me. *So that's why she likes the story so much,* I thought. I didn't feel strange, just kinda happy that Lilly could somehow feel "healed" like Lazarus at the end of the story. But that night I found out identifying with Lazarus wasn't all happiness for Lilly.

Grandpa had come home early from his rounds. I was sitting on his lap like a three-year-old, hearing "Little Red Riding Hood" again. I didn't care though. He enjoyed it and so did I. Grandma Melissee had dropped her big iron kettle on the floor. Afterwards she blamed herself for having waked Lilly. But Grandpa said, "Now she's had these spells before. The wind must have blown the light out."

We heard such a horrible shrill scream that at first I thought it was a cat fight. But Grandpa knew right away—it was Lilly. Grandma and I rushed in Lilly's room after Grandpa. Grandpa grabbed her hands first. Lilly's face was scratched and she was screaming, "Unwrap my face so I can breathe! I'm not dead! Open the tomb!" Her whole body was writhing, but her feet and legs stayed next to each other like the pictures of Egyptian mummies I had seen in my geography book.

Grandpa tied her hands to the bed and then shook her shoulders, "Lilly! Lilly! You're not Lazarus! You're Lilly." Lilly kept screaming. "It does no good," Grandpa said, turning to look at me. "She'll just have to wear herself out. We'll have to keep the light on for her."

Grandpa closed the door and said, "Come with me, Ina." We walked down the hall to Grandpa's medicine room. I had never seen it before. "Look at all this, Ina. My shelves are full of tonics and potions." Grandpa picked up a small green bottle. "Yet none of these medicines can help my Lilly. These are for sickness in the body, not in the mind."

Grandpa never kept this room locked. Since he always made house calls, there was only Grandma around. So it was easy to sneak in while Grandpa was away. I was determined to write down the name of every medicine he had on his shelves. Beside each name, I copied the sickness it was supposed to cure.

For sore throats there was golden seal, a fine brown powder which looked like dirt and kerosene. That smell just about made me throw up. Syrup of squills made me think it was made from porcupine. The directions on the bottle read, "For phlegm caused from croup and whooping cough." I wondered if Ma had used any of this on Everett.

I thought cream of tartar was for cooking, but Grandpa had written on the label, "For bloating when pregnant." I pictured myself being all puffed up like the posters I had seen of the fat lady in the circus. When I got married I was going to get the biggest can of cream of tartar I could find.

A whole pile of clean cloths were at the end of the shelf. *Grandpa's poultices* I thought. Next to them there was a big jar with the word "asiphidita" on it. It sounded so familiar that I thought I'd take a smell. It was so awful I barely got the top back on before I thought I'd faint. I ran out of the room and outside to the barn. Now I remembered. Kids wore that around their neck to school when they had colds. Nanny Allen made them sit in the back of the room, but you could still smell them no matter where you sat.

Anyhow, Lilly didn't have any more "spells" while I was there. We just went on with me, pretending to be Lazarus' sister Mary, and Lilly, thinking she was Lazarus.

I'd spend my time away from Lilly thinking about all the people I'd miraculously cure in my lifetime. I'd hope I had "healing fingers" like Grandma said Grandpa had. I'd picture Lilly becoming well the last day I was there. I'd be the talk of the state. Maybe even somebody rich would send me to medical school. I even began to pray again. It seemed right to pray because, of course, God wanted Lilly to be well. But nothing happened and it was time to leave. School started in a couple weeks and I had to go home. I was really glad in a way. Although I liked Grandpa, and he and Grandma tried to be as cheerful as they could, playing Mary and Lazarus all the time got me down.

Lilly decided she wanted to go to the train to see me off. Grandpa was glad because usually Lilly never wanted to go out. I was glad, too, because this was one last chance for God to heal Lilly before I left. The ride to the train seemed long. Lilly stared straight ahead, saying nothing. When the sun came out from behind the clouds, Grandpa began to sweat. Lilly blinked and reached for my hand. Her hand was as cold as always.

I still remember how Lilly looked as the train pulled away—her white face under her black bonnet perfectly still against the green cottonwoods and the blue summer sky. It was like the old black-and-white pictures Ma had of unsmiling faces against the blue-and-pink-flowered wallpaper of her bedroom. They didn't fit and neither did Lilly. She was in her tomb already.

The next winter when we heard about Lilly's death, I wasn't surprised. To me Lilly had already died. I had done my crying over Lilly the first few days I was at Grandpa's house. I didn't think about her again until the spring.

Ma had been bragging about her lily that had bloomed right on Easter when Pa came in the next morning with doom written on his face, "Ma, we had a frost last night and your flower didn't make it." Ma held it in her hand for a while saying, "The dark earth just froze out its roots—so lily white." I pressed it in my Bible, but when it got all brown and crumbly like fall leaves I threw it away.

CHAPTER 4

Summer, 1896

AFTER BEING AT GRANDPA MARTIN'S, I didn't mind if the rest of the summer was ordinary. In fact, I hoped it would be. But I was wrong.

Soon after I was home, Ma sent me in the house to get Pa a clean shirt. He was going into town and needed to get there before the store closed, so I was to take a shirt to him out where he was plowing in the heat. He would change out there. While I was getting the shirt off its hanger, I noticed a big box stuck 'way back in the corner. That box puzzled me. It was too early for Christmas presents to be hidden around the house.

'Course, the first thing I did when I came in was to go straight to Pa's closet and open that box. Well, there were just some old, yellow letters. I was disappointed, but then I thought, *I'm ten years old. That's old enough to understand people's private thoughts*. The letters were all addressed to Martha Wilson, Pa's mother, who had died after he was grown, from her husband, Milton, Pa's dad.

The letters were tied with string and from the looks of the postmarks, were arranged according to date— earliest to latest. Before reading the first one, I looked for the closing signature. Yep, it was Milton. I wasn't just sure if I should be reading 'em, but I didn't want to take a chance on asking Pa's permission (in case he'd say no). I took them down to a place where I was sure no one would find me—Orchard Pond—and wedged myself in between some huckleberry bushes that were tall enough to cover me. It was a favorite hiding spot for hide-and-seek 'cause nobody could see anybody in there! The bushes kinda settled around you as if they were helping you hide. This spot had another advantage. If you got hungry waiting there for someone to find you, you could just reach up and drop a huckleberry in your mouth.

My problem was getting the letters out of the house without being seen. I took the first few letters and carefully tied them around my waist under my dress. Except for a little crackling sound, which I was sure only I could hear, nobody could tell a thing. When I got settled in my spot, I opened the first letter.

November 5, 1861

My Dearest Martha,

My bride of five months, I would greet you with a long embrace, but under present conditions, I can only greet you with, "My Dearest Martha." You are the dearest in the world to me. I see that more clearly with every day that passes without a glimpse of you and with every mile that takes me farther away from your arms.

We did not imagine, my sweetest love, that when I proposed over a year ago a great and terrible war would tear us apart. Of course, the whole country is torn apart and many are dying—brothers killed by brothers (all men are brothers) but what bleeds my heart is the violence done to us. No, I am not hurt, not in any way that can be seen. The wound I carry is deeper and, therefore, cannot be patched with white linen or dug out, like a bullet. Our souls which have grown as one have now been forced to become two. The jagged scars left by our parting never heal, but each moment pains me more, especially now that you are with child, our child.

I know you must be distressed, having no word from me. A month has passed since I left for St. Louis to serve under Fremont, but there was no possibility of getting a letter to you until now. We have been on the move, chasing Price down to Springfield. It has been a sad march, seeing the empty homes and the fields stripped bare and scorched. I am so thankful to know that my dear ones are safe (for now I have two dear ones) and out of the line of march.

Marching down to Springfield began as a rather jovial lot. One would have thought to hear our whistlings and see our smiles that we were in a Fourth of July parade. The weather was fine—cool but sunny. But it was no parade, as we discovered at our first fight in Fredericktown. A few men were killed on both sides. Fortunately, I was not at the forefront. I am in deep dread of the day I shall have to shoot the rifle at my side, not at any deer, but at another man, someone's husband or son.

Our second fight was at Springfield and involved more men, though not all 38,000. I did fire twice, but the enemy was too distant to hit (for which I am thankful). After Springfield, General Price agreed to surrender. The officers under him stationed at Wilson's Creek would not give in. We were told to prepare for battle. As we were lining up, the message passed down the line that Fremont had been relieved by General Hunter and ordered by President Lincoln to withdraw the troops.

So we await marching orders. Everyone's a bit confused. Some of the men are mad as a goat in a bees' nest. They're the ones that are itching for a fight. Me, I feel relieved, but I wouldn't admit it to anyone but you, Martha.

And now, my dearest, how do you fare? I hope you are not still feeling ill in the mornings.

I pray for you when daylight pales,
I pray for you to never fail
In your love for me
And I for thee.

Your Milton

We have just heard we will be camped at Rollo. Please address a letter to me there.

I read the closing again. I sure wished I'd get letters like that someday. When I came to the parts about the war, I read faster. They didn't interest me half as much as the love parts, which I read over and over. I ate some more huckleberries and opened the second letter.

December 24, 1861

My Dear Wife,

I was so happy to get your letter, which I have devoured, as well as your Christmas gift, which I could not wait to open. I am glad that I did not wait, as we have had early frosts and the socks and mittens have kept me warm. Even more important to me is knowing that your beloved hands have fashioned every stitch. At the same time, I can't help feeling sorry for those less fortunate than myself, whose hands and toes are continually frozen. In the best of times, a diet of hardtack and hog-meat is bad enough, but under the present conditions, it is unbearable.

My poor dear! I have done nothing but complain about myself, while you must be feeling extremely discomforted, being alone with child. I was glad to hear of your sister coming for the holidays. Christmas shall be a lonely affair for all of us. The pain of being away from you has not lessened. One merely learns to live with it, as Charlie lives with his wooden leg.

Have I told you of Charlie yet? He lost his leg fighting Indians out West, where he volunteered for this war. The only thing they'd give him to do was cooking. We all say he stirs those big pots with his leg. He's a pleasant fellow and cheers us all up plenty.

There has been no fighting but plenty of deaths. Some soldiers joke about it being safer on the battlefield than in the camp. We laugh, but it's no joke to those who lie six feet under in this frozen ground. Death is everywhere alike.

We are awaiting orders to march. Away from you my heart is frozen as solid as the ground we stomp over. It, too, is awaiting orders so it may love again.

Until I see your face,
Milton

February 18, 1862

My Fairest Lily,

It is right that I should address you thus. Remember the first flower we picked together was a white lily? White lilies in May—and ever after it was our flower and May was our month. When you were a bride, you wore them as a garland in your hair. As you walked closer to me for our vows, their delicious scent filled the air. I have only to close my eyes for a moment and I am transported back in time to that lovely May day.

Gazing on your face so white and fair
While lilies danced in your dark hair,
Your breath gave sweet perfume to every kiss,
But it is the softness of your arms that I miss.

If our child that is born in May is a girl, we must surely name her Lily. If he is a boy, I thought Thomas Milton would be nice. I hope you have not tried to write, as we have moved from Rollo and now are at Sugar Creek, some 210 miles from Rollo and 320 miles from St. Louis.

General Curtis is our commander now. On January 9th we left for Lebanon and expected to be moved any day. At Lebanon I suffered badly from a deep chest cold. I feared it was pneumonia. But this is to explain my long absence from the pen. I feel my resistance to disease is lower than it has ever been. Charlie, that wise old codger, says camp is bad for soldiers—too much time on their hands, plus worn bodies and heartsick loneliness. When you're fighting, Charlie says you forget about all your pains inside and out. Then the cause becomes the thing that matters.

At any rate, we are on the move now, having left Lebanon the 10th of February for Marshfield on the 11th and arriving at McPherson's Creek on the 12th. There was a slight skirmish with the enemy to the rear of our troops. Many of us didn't know it had occurred till it was over. Some of our men were wounded, but none seriously. On the 13th we marched back into Springfield. It would have made you weep, Martha, to see the condition of that beautiful city—the gardens, especially. All the trees which lined the streets were ravished and only stumps left—used for firewood, I expect. Most of the houses were deserted. I was glad to stay only a few hours. Springfield will forever remain a scar in my memory, a wounded and bleeding city.

We left that night, splitting into two columns, one under General Sigel. Mine went under Curtis. We planned to meet at McDowell's. We arrived first, so Curtis said we had the pleasure of driving out our unwanted houseguests—Price's rear guard. Again there was not much bloodshed, as we vastly outnumbered them. After a few shots, they beat a hasty retreat. Sigel's column joined us and we proceeded together on to Cassville, Keetsville, and Elkhorn Tavern, arriving at Sugar Creek today. We plan to advance 12 miles farther south to Cross Hollows.

I would not advise that you write me, as we shall not be here long. We are chasing Price, you see, hoping for a confrontation that will end this war in Missouri. That is what the officers are hoping for. I am hoping to return home to my bride after being away from her arms.

Pray for me. I am anxious for battle only because it must be before I can return home. May angels watch over my most precious possession on earth.

Milton

April 10, 1862

My Springtime Love,

I had almost forgotten what season it is. Everything has been so brown since I joined in October. Brown leaves gave way to frozen, brown mud and then, when the rains came, the mud flowed free. It has all been the same season—the season of death. Now, in sitting down to write and to gaze at the blue sky, I see green buds on the trees and I see your hair wreathed with lilies.

I know you have worried, my love, and rightly so, for

many times death has come to those in front of me or on either side of me; yet I have not suffered even a scratch! I have God to thank for that and the sweet prayers of my angelic wife. For surely you are an angel to me and would be a far more welcome vision than any heavenly messenger!

So much has happened that it seems 20 years since I wrote you last, 50 years since I left the contentment of our farm.

At the beginning of March, the men all split up to various locations to watch for Price. I went with the division under Sigel to McKissick's farm. On the night of the 5th, we heard Price was approaching the next day. He had hoped to catch us by surprise, but General Curtis sent us the message of his whereabouts. We were to leave at two the next morning. I can assure you that not many of us slept that night! Old Charlie was beside himself with excitement. I hope you won't call me cold-hearted if I say he hadn't much to lose. He has no family and already is maimed. I felt no excitement, only dread and small stirrings, wanting to run through the dark woods and hide. Charlie said all that is natural to feel before a first, big battle.

At 2:00 A.M. we marched to Sugar Creek, where all the divisions were concentrating. There we lay in wait. That, I believe, was the worst, not knowing if this were our last day on earth. I tried to write to you then, but only succeeded in adding more kindling to the fire with my torn papers.

Toward dawn we were awakened with the news that the noise of the wagons and artillery had been heard on the back road, but no one had seen the troops. They began attacking our left flank. Two of Price's generals—McCullock and McIntosh—were killed. This threw their men into confusion and they retreated to Elkhorn Tavern. The right flank, attacked by Price himself, did not fare as well. They were forced to retreat into the woods.

We began moving that afternoon. We moved very slowly so as not to give away our position and did not arrive till early evening to provide reinforcements to our right flank. We lay that night on the open field, our guns beside us, with no campfires allowed, lest they betray our position. About midnight, we had orders to move back to camp, where we would have food and blankets. Sigel had spotted the enemy, enjoying his own campfires, and was assured they would not attack till morning.

The next morning on the 8th, we marched back to the same, open field. About seven o'clock we began advancing in lines. We looked a bit like hide-and-seek players, running quickly between the tall grasses and then crouching down again on our bellies. The cannons' roar was in our ears. It was hard to judge how near the balls were coming. When we got closer to Price's men, we shot, lying on our bellies, directing our fire to a high spur of the hills where the enemy hid behind rocks and boulders. Our men soon closed in around the ridge on three sides, forcing them to flee. We then rushed to pursue them down the other side of Pea Ridge.

That was the end of the battle. I stood straight and looked up for the first time since it had began. The sun was directly overhead. What seemed like days had been less than six hours.

When the roll call was taken that night, over a thousand men did not answer. The silence after their names were called remains their only memorial. Only 203 bodies were found. The wounded lay around us, bleeding and moaning. *Are these the trophies of war?* I thought. We had won, but no one felt like celebrating. Even Charlie seemed to have lost his excitement. No one even talked. We were as silent as we had been before the battle. Each man was alone with his own thoughts. There was no back-slapping or handshaking on the victor's side, nor did anyone repeat the conquests of the day. Such things are for schoolboys and Sunday picnickers. This was no game. The prizes were much higher than a cake or a kiss. To win meant more of us were alive, but alive for what? The next fight?

There are rumors that the Indians under Price engaged in tomahawking, but from the bodies I've seen, there was no evidence of the sort.

The Battle of Pea Ridge is over for us as you read with joy my letter and know that I am safe. But for those mothers and sweethearts who receive the black-bordered envelopes, it will continue for the rest of their lives. I have much more I could tell you, but I will save this till I am home, hopefully in May, *our* month, for the birth of Lily or Thomas Milton (or maybe both!)

A grateful
Milton

That was all the letters that fit under my waist, so I filled in the next few months in my mind. I knew he'd come home, 'cause Pa was born May 6 and Pa said his father held him when he was only a few days old. I suppose he said, with a smile on his face, 'We'll call the next one Lily.' I imagined their joy at greeting, Martha with her new babe in her arms, walking toward Milton still far off. Milton had served his time, Pa said, and she expected he'd be home till they died—old in their beds.

I imagined, too, that fateful day in August when the gentleman rider came to offer Milton a small fortune to serve his time for him. Pa said Milton thought he could pay off the farm with it and even buy a bigger one. Pa said it must have been a tempting sum, one that would have taken twenty years of farming to save up. Anyway, he left again and my tearful parting scene ended in my mind, with Martha watching his figure grow smaller and smaller.

My stomach turned over, telling me it was time for supper. So, tying the letters up again, and hiding them under my skirt, I started for home.

CHAPTER 5

Early morning

THE NEXT DAY I GOT AN early start, remembering to bring a sandwich with me. As I walked, I happily patted the letters under my dress. I had taken all the rest of them and stuck them on both sides.

When I got to the bushes, I piled up some huckleberries in front of me. They looked to me like small cannon balls waiting to be fired. Then I opened the next letter.

September 10, 1862

To My Two Darlings,

I have arrived safely to find that a new General—Schofield—is in command. Our troops have swollen to 50,000. Springfield looks a little brighter than last winter. People have moved back and planted their gardens and new saplings stand beside the stumps. The people are very friendly to us. I take it they feel safer with so many soldiers present.

I am already deep in the pain of separation, but what other choice did I have? With the Confederacy holding the Mississippi, we see farmers all around burning their corn for fuel. Without the gentleman's check, you, too, should starve. We must put the health of our dear baby son first, above our own happiness. This separation is so short compared to the lifetime we will have together. The thoughts of our future is what sustains me.

This Indian summer may be pleasant to those who live in fine houses, but for us who live with wood ticks, chiggers, and bedbugs, it is a curse. We pray for the first frost to kill our unwanted companions. But for now we do have all the vegetables and fruit we can eat. We will be sorry when our diet returns to hardtack and hogmeat. Some of the younger, unmarried soldiers got their eye on a pretty Springfield lass. Many of the troops are new— their uniforms, freshly starched by some mother or sister and their buttons polished. So the girls respond! "War is not so bad," I hear many of them remark after strolling around Springfield with the delicate Southern belles on their arm. " 'Course, they have not fought," Charlie and I remind each other. Charlie is still here, hobbling about, busier than ever.

The cavalry has orders to chase the Confederate guerillas out of Missouri—orders to burn, kill, and destroy. I'm glad to be in the infantry, but we, ourselves, are waiting to attack.

My darling, kiss Milton for me. I'm glad you have him for company. Tell him his father says he has the best mother in the world.

Milton

November 21, 1862

Dearest Martha and Thomas Milton,

We have a new general—Blount is his name. He's 36 and was a doctor in Ohio before signing up. Schofield has returned to St. Louis because of illness. He had quite a busy fall, as we did who went with him, but more of this later.

Having been gone away from Springfield nearly two months, I found two letters waiting for me. You must remember that if you fail to receive a letter for a while, do not be distressed because I am all right. If I am missing or injured or the worst, you should receive a letter informing you of my fate.

I'm happy to hear Thomas Milton's first tooth has arrived successfully, even if it wasn't quietly. As for his continual smile, I'd expect as much from a baby who has such a beautiful face to gaze upon each day.

No, it was not too early to send the scarf. The first frost is here and the bedbugs have succumbed to the elements.

I am so glad you are both well and that your sister has moved near you. With your parents there for the holidays, Thomas Milton will have an appreciative audience for his antics. To think of another Thanksgiving and Christmas away from you is more than I can bear. I have endured cold and sweat and hunger, but loneliness is the cruelest hardship of all. Those others only affect a man's body. Loneliness eats into the soul. A fire can warm cold limbs; a cool breeze relieves the heat; even hardtack and beans can soothe the stomach, but the cure for loneliness is kept from me. I cannot linger any longer in this vein or I shall surely be shot as a deserter.

Now I'll tell you of my activities. At the end of September, some of us marched with Schofield to Newtonia to assist General Salomon, who had been driven back by four or five thousand Indians and white troops. We then pursued the Confederates out of Missouri and into the

48

mountains of Arkansas. They were going to take a stand near Fayetteville where we attacked on the 27th of October. They retreated to the banks of the Arkansas and we returned to Springfield.

Chasing men through forests and mountains, like hunting wild deer, is a miserable occupation. Fortunately, they stayed far enough ahead of us to escape any large losses. Sometimes we'd hurry them on with some gunshots. Charlie would have said we were filling their britches with buckshot, but I don't think out bullets got that close. We passed some of their dead. Seems they died mostly from disease or exhaustion. While they didn't have time to bury their own, we did. One in our ranks was a preacher, and the way he talked over those dead Confederates, you would have never known they were the enemy but thought they were his brothers, and so he was somebody's brother.

I asked the preacher after the service if we weren't responsible for enemy deaths. I wanted to know if war was a special situation where God could lift the rules that he'd laid down in the Good Book. The preacher said, "No, war isn't special. God's rules are the same." He drew me aside and in a whisper said, "Sometimes I fire my rifle into the air or above the trees." Now I've always fired right into the enemy lines, but I've never seen my bullet hit anyone. 'Course, maybe it did. Only if I shot in the air like the preacher could I be sure I'd never killed anyone. I prayed then and there that God would forgive me and vowed to be a worst shot in future fights. I know you pray, too, Martha, and that's why I'm still alive. I shall write more as soon as I can. Waiting your reply, your loving husband and father,

Milton

My Darlings,

It is a new year but only more of the same. There was no celebrating here. Thomas Milton's present of the ear-muffs was most appreciated. Do thank him for me. I'm wearing them now.

We missed being attacked on December 7th due only to the Confederates' learning of our reinforcements coming. Hindman had driven our pickets on December 6th and was planning to attack the next night. Blount had learned of Hindman's plans on the 24th of November, so he had sent for General Herron and 6,000 more men. When Herron was still 12 miles away from Blount, Hindman attacked him. Hindman would have had the victory, but after attacking with his calvary, he waited to bring up his infantry until Herron attacked him. When Herron attacked, Blount was close enough to hear his guns, so we rushed in to assist Herron. We fought all day. There were a lot more of us than them. During the night, Hindman retreated. They're calling it the Battle of Prairie Grove. Herron lost 918 men and we lost, under Blount, 333.

On the 28th we attacked the retreating Confederates (to hasten their retreat, Charlie said).

I cannot tell you what I think about under fire. It seems as if I don't think at all. I feel very much like a fox smoked out of his hole, forced into the open to run for his life. Only we must not only run, but shoot at the same time. But then a fox generally knows who his pursuer is and how close he is coming to the hound. We never do know. There is always the stray bullet, the unlucky volley that lands in the midst of our troops and stills some forever. If I were to tell you of the horrible disfigurements I have seen (I can no longer call them men), both living and dead, you would vomit as many of us have. I do not say this to scare you, as I believe with all my heart I shall live and return to you. As a matter of fact, I have come to a great conclusion from the suffering I have observed: I should rather die outright than be disfigured in any way. I have heard the screams from medical tents and seen the piles of arms and legs outside the door. I have sworn no part of me shall ever be added to that pile. Besides, most of the men die of infection after the surgery, anyway. Charlie was one of the lucky few.

Enough of this gloom. I have my mittens, my socks, my earmuffs, and my dear wife and son at home. What more could any man desire (under the present circumstances)? After every victory, we say, "Surely this war cannot last," and we all talk of spring planting as if we were going home tomorrow. But we shall have our month of May together, of that I am sure.

Yours,
Milton

March 15, 1863

My Lily and Her Small Flower,

Hindman's army has all but dissipated, with only 10,000 of the Confederates left in camp at Little Rock. We were all wild with excitement when we heard there was no one left to fight in Missouri, but it did not last long. Schofield requested troops be sent to Grant at Vicksburg, Mississippi. Curtis said no, that all 45,000 men were needed to make sure no Southern sympathizers were about. Well, the Governor agreed with Curtis, and Schofield resigned. Curtis' troop-hoarding reached President Lincoln, who appointed General Sumner to replace him. But Sumner died on the way here. So we are without a general. "Maybe that means we can go home," someone suggested. But rumor has it that Schofield will be reappointed. Charlie said, "Nobody is gonna let 45,000 men go home with war raging in the East."

Charlie's right. We have all heard that the war will last well into the summer. Now our hopes are set on a leave. I see nothing to prevent it. While they are deciding who should lead us and where we should be led to would be the perfect time to let us all attend to our fields and families.

The rich bear the worst of the war. I have seen men I served with in '61 who have walked home to a charred house, or one stripped bare of all furniture and even staircases. It seems if you are poor, you are no special target for the enemy. They have less than the poorest of our neighbors. My little wife and son are well cared for, while others' families are forced to beg and live in abject poverty.

There is not much more news. I hope this is my last letter until I return to see you. We shall celebrate Thomas Milton's first birthday and I expect to see his first step then, also.

Kiss each other for me,
Milton

May 20, 1863

My Dearest Treasures,

I have waited so long to write because I believed at any day I would be walking down the road towards home, with lilies that I gathered on the way to present to you, but all has changed.

Schofield is in command now and 30,000 march to Vicksburg to join General Grant in battle. If we win, they say the war will be over, but I no longer believe them.

This has been a despondent month for me, the worst since the war began. I would gladly repay all the money given me to take the gentleman's place in war, if I could take his—sitting each meal with his family, sleeping each night with his wife. I have missed our son's first birthday, I have missed endless affections from the darling of my life, and no money can repay me for what I have lost.

The mere sight of a lily in the forest sends me into tears until Charlie thinks I am hopelessly shell-shocked. Maybe I am, but my disease is only curable by a glimpse of those I hold most dear. To have just a day in your presence, a morning or an hour, would be enough, but even that little time is denied me. We shall always speak of this month with sadness as the May we lost and the lilies we did not gather.

I need your prayers
Milton

Thus ended my morning's reading. I stopped to eat my sandwich in between huckleberries. I was feeling sad about Milton not seeing Martha, as if it were now instead of thirty-three years ago. I wanted to go to that General Schofield and demand that he let Milton go home. Of course, these feelings were silly. The war was over and most everyone who fought on either side was dead.

After my last bite, I began to read again.

July 10, 1863

To the Bright and Shining Lights of my Life,

The greeting is not exaggerated. I have been in a great, black pit since I last wrote. It doesn't seem fair that you receive such letters of woe in reply to your delightful accounts of Thomas Milton's newest words and actions. Thank you for teaching him to say, "Papa" from my picture, but how sad that it must be from a picture and not from my own person!

I did receive your letter in Vicksburg. This was to be

the biggest battle I'd been in and my first one without Charlie. I never realized how much it helped me to tell my feelings to Charlie. We thought he might be sent along to cook for some of the 30,000 men being sent, but his wooden leg is only suited for walking from the fire to the dining tent. He didn't seem disappointed at not being able to come. Even Charlie has had enough of war.

Vicksburg was the last Confederate stronghold on the Mississippi. A victory there meant the Mississippi would be opened to the North.

We arrived at Vicksburg on June 11th under General Herron and camped on the Big Black River to the left of Grant's troops. We now numbered 71,000, spread out along the eight roads leading to Vicksburg. We camped in between the Confederates under Pemberton and Johnson. On June 22nd we received the news that Johnson had crossed the river for the purpose of attacking our rear guard and joining up with Pemberton. Grant gave Sherman the command of all the forces from Haynes' Bluff to the Big Black River. We were to wait and attack when Sherman needed reinforcements.

Johnson did not attack. Seeing the size of our troops no doubt caused him to change his mind. Since we'd arrived we had been steadily pushing forward toward Vicksburg. A ditch had been dug right up to the Confederate fort on the Jackson Road. The dirt was piled on both sides of the ditch to create two parapets. Over this parapet, some of our Union soldiers exchanged bread for cigarettes with the Confederate troops, and conversed. At other times, the enemy would throw hand grenades at us. Our men would catch them and throw them back.

The purpose of the ditch was to plant a mine under the fort. The Confederates did not discover the mine. It exploded on June 25th. The men in the fort were thrown into the air and some of them, still alive, came down on our side. One man said he thought he flew nearly a mile high! Part of our troops jumped into the crater where the fort had been. This proved foolish, as they were easy targets for grenades, and 30 were killed.

On the 21st of June we heard that Pemberton was planning to escape at night across the river. He had hired workmen to build boats for this purpose, pulling down houses to secure the lumber. We heard later that his rebel army had wanted him to surrender, but he had refused. The river was so closely watched that escape for him became impossible.

On July 1st we were within 100 yards of the enemy. The attack was to be July 6th. About ten o'clock on July 3rd, two Confederates came toward us waving white flags, and bearing a message of surrender. We were jubilant. We were having our Fourth celebration early! Our celebrations were short-lived as we discovered Pemberton did not wish to surrender unconditionally as Grant demanded, but wanted a cease-fire so his troops could march out. Pemberton and Grant had served with the same division in the Mexican War. Grant said he would send a list of his final terms that night to Pemberton. He did so and Pemberton replied and then Grant replied again. They were haggling over terms. When Pemberton finally agreed to surrender, he was to display white flags. The morning of July 4th, they were there!

We were all jubilant—dancing jigs and calling to the "Johnnies" across the line while they called to us "Yanks"! When they marched out of Vicksburg to surrender their arms, we held our cheers. We shared our bread with the very soldiers we had been trying to starve out! When Fort Huron heard Vicksburg had surrendered, they did the same. The entire Mississippi was in Northern hands.

It took a full week to sign prison paroles from the Union for Pemberton's men. On the 11th of July, they marched out. Most of them deserted and returned to their families, which is what Grant had hoped they would do. Over 31,000 men had surrendered. The enemies' muskets were far superior to our large flintlocks, so we exchanged our old ones for their weapons.

Though our skirmishes cost us over 1,000 men, considering the size of our army, had we fought, our losses would have been much greater.

General Grant's son, not quite 13, is here with him. I should not like Thomas Milton ever to be involved in war, even when he is twice the age of Grant's son. Maybe our different feelings about the war are the reason he is a general and I am merely an infantryman (and content to remain so).

You cannot imagine how relieved I feel about the outcome of the prospective battle. However, there was no talk of being sent home this time. We knew Grant would hang on to every man till the total victory was secured. We are just moved around like chess pieces until the game is over.

Grant has ordered our troops under Herron to report to Banks, who has come to consult with Grant. We have heard they both wish to attack Mobile. Do not write to me there until you hear more definite plans.

Maybe I am safe because your prayers laid siege against Vicksburg. They certainly turned the heart of Pemberton,

Milton

Martha, My Love,

We are back in New Orleans awaiting orders. I have marched many miles since I wrote last. Instead of marching on Mobile as we had expected, Banks was ordered to Texas. Texas! How far I am from the ones I love. I had hoped to see Texas some day, but only from the windows of a pleasant train car, not from the crowded transports of war. From New Orleans we sailed to Sabine Pass, where the river reaches the gulf. The plan was to move in and occupy Houston, which would give us control of the railroad. The reasons we were ordered to Texas are not to do with the war, itself. Napoleon III, Emperor of France, taking advantage of our country being at war, sent French troops to take Mexico in June. The federal government was afraid the Confederates weren't strong enough to hold Texas. They planned to drive out the Confederates first and then establish defenses against the French.

We all agreed with Grant and Blount that it was a mistake. Our forces could have swept Mobile and the rest of the South, ending the war. As it was, Grant's force was too small to do anything. He could only wait on us to finish in Texas.

We were finished in Texas sooner than we thought. On September 8th our gunboats moved up the river to attack the Confederate fort. One boat was shot through her boilers, the second boat ran aground and was shot, and the other two boats retreated. We turned around and went back to New Orleans, my second battle avoided. If I could wait the rest of the war out this way, my chances are good to come to you.

We have been sent back to Blount, to our camp on the banks of the Arkansas. Charlie and I had a tearful reunion. In some ways he has taken the place of my own, dead father and I, the son he never had. Charlie said he was surprised I was still alive. I replied, "I'm not, having missed both battles I was to fight in." Charlie enjoyed hearing my news and had some of his own.

I'm sure you've heard of the murder of the 150 citizens in Lawrence, Kansas, by Quantrill's raiders last August. The news made me sick with fear that it would continue into other towns. Of course, the capture of Fort Smith and Little Rock by our troops has secured the whole area, but Quantrill's raiders are still at large and I cannot rest.

Little Rock was another battle not fought. Our casualties were incurred when the stragglers from Price's retreat turned around to fire on us. Even so, 55 dead is small in comparison to other battles. (I am talking coldly now like a general.) Of course, no death is small. The Good Book says God sees whenever a sparrow falls.

As we approached Little Rock, Price's men were occupying the trenches on the north side of the Arkansas River in order to prevent our crossing. One of our troop under Davidson did get across. When Price learned of the crossing, he evacuated Little Rock.

So it has been some time since I have been under fire or forced to fire. The preacher wouldn't even have to shoot in the air in my case. He would be most happy with this state of affairs, as I am. I don't know where he is—perhaps he was hired to preach Confederate funerals, if so he will make a fair living. I have long since lost track of him.

I am in need of another pair of socks and mittens for the winter. If you cannot get to it, I shall understand. Thomas Milton keeps you busy, I judge from your letters.

Longing for home,
Milton

On the top of the next letter was printed a poem;

The Voice of Her I Love

How sweet at close of silent eve
The harp's responsive sound;
How sweet the vows that ne'er deceive,
And deeds by virtue crown'd!
How sweet to sit beneath a tree
In some delightful grove;
But oh! more soft, more sweet to me,
The voice of her I love.

Whene'er she joins the village train
to hail the newborn day,
Mellifluous note compose each strain
Which zephyrs waft away.
The frowns of fate I'll calmly bear;
In humble sphere to move,
Content and bless'd where e'er I hear
The voice of her I love.

November 18, 1863

Dear Wife,

This evening finds me in good health and hoping you and the boy are the same. I have some leisure time and wanted to fill it by writing to you.

A sad incident happened last Saturday. A lieutenant and his men were scouting not far from here, where they met a rebel band. The rebels fired and killed two men and captured the lieutenant, saying the rebels would exchange him for another prisoner. The prisoner was delivered and the lieutenant was delivered, too—dead. The rebels claimed it was self-defense, that he stole a rifle and started shooting, but we don't believe anything of the kind.

Every morning I look at your miniature, that was taken on our wedding day. The lilies never fade from your hair and your smile never fades—so like our love.

I tried to get my picture taken to send to you, but could

not get one that suited me. You are all the world to me. My mind is ever with you and my prayer to God is that we may live once more together on earth and forever in the upper world. I am glad you live as a Christian. I intend to live the best I can under my circumstances.

On October 6th, 80 of our men were wounded and then fell into Quantrill's hands! On the 13th Shelby's raiders and Quantrill's raiders were defeated, so both bands shall trouble Missouri no more.

Your
Milton

January 10, 1864

My Dear Ones,

Another Christmas has passed without you. Since our marriage, we have not spent one together. We have many happy memories to make when the war is over! I'm glad to hear Thomas Milton enjoyed his presents. The entire check *was* for toys. The train, top, and ball were all gifts I never had and next year he shall have the best toy of all—his Papa! I spend hours thinking of the times we shall have, fishing and swimming together. When he is older, he will no doubt farm. I shall teach him all I can.

This winter seems drearier than last. The camp blankets are made of shoddy material, which we discovered is the refuse and wood shavings from manufacturing shops—pounded, rolled, and glued. It is not real cloth and falls to pieces when wet.

Everyone seems to be sick—sick enough to apply for a sick leave but not sick enough to die. No one wants Chickahoming or camp fever as this falls into the latter category, but there would be a long line if mumps were handed out.

This winter, because of its severity, has kept both sides—Confederate and Union—around their campfires.

We know they have it worse than we do. At least, our hogmeat never runs out. The coffin makers are as busy as if we were engaged in battle. The Doctor told me he believes twice as many men die in camp as in battle.

There are rumors we will join Banks after his return from Texas to take the Red River in Arkansas and that we will attack Mobile at last. Of course, there are always those rumors that we shall go home, but nobody believes them anymore.

You and Thomas Milton seem so far away, as if life with you was a pleasant dream. Upon awakening, I find the real situation is the suspended world of sorrow and routine. Every death has become part of that routine. Please don't think me callous by saying that I no longer feel as I did about looking on corpses. This change on my part I would have condemned in another man, but now I see it is necessary for survival. If one spends all his waking hours mourning, one is likely to join these frozen ghosts.

I for one have not even a sniffle, thanks to my new purple socks and mittens. Of course, the men snickered at first when I put them on, but after I explained that my infant son selected the color, they enjoyed seeing me wear them. My purple mittens have brightened up the gloom by bringing memories of home to all of us. Thank you.

May the future hold all that we wish,
Laced with a sweet kiss
To my lady so fair
With lilies in her hair.

Milton

March 15, 1864

My May-time Loves,

We have a new commander now—General Rosecrans, a most interesting fella. Rosecrans is a hard worker, never retiring before 2:00 and sometimes not till 4:00. His young aides have a time keeping up with him. Yet he is so kind we have taken to calling him, "Old Rosey." During inspection, if a soldier has worn-out shoes or ragged breeches, he sends him to the captain to get what he needs. His optimism is just what we need. Charlie says the sound of his voice alone is enough to thaw the ice on the puddles.

We expect to be joining Banks at the Red River any day. They had hoped to get down it by now with their troops but the river is too shallow. Usually by this time of year it is overflowing.

I have decided that if the war is not over by spring, I shall write to the gentleman and ask him to release me from my obligations. Perhaps he can find another farmer to come in for him. I for one can no longer bear this useless separation. I suppose the war-makers should be most offended at my choice of the word *useless*, but the longer the war goes on, the more clearly I see that the purpose of life is to love and be loved, to raise children to fear God and to care for one's own. War is not man's glorious calling to a higher purpose, but only an interruption in the everyday glory of living—an irritation like a mosquito bite or a speck of dust in your eye. I shall soon wipe the smudge away from my life and return to sleeping on clean sheets and watching you awaken in the morning sunlight. I shall be glad to have Thomas Milton climb over me every day as if he were scaling a mountain. I should not mind any of his antics. He may pull my hair until it all falls out, so glad I shall be to see him!

I *shall* see you this May. If the gentleman does not release me of my obligation, I know "Old Rosey" will grant a leave to a man who has been in over 18 months!

Until our next embrace,
Milton

After this letter, I just filled in what happened next in my mind.

Pa had told me many times how he and his Ma hid behind the door that May day so they could jump out and surprise Milton. Martha had had a dream that Milton would be coming home the next day, hobbling on a cane, but still coming home.

So she and Pa waited and waited. Finally they walked out to look for him. I'd wondered how long they stood at that fence watching the road before they gave up and went back in the house. It was May 12.

The last letter was in a different handwriting. Instead of Milton's evenly slanted script, the letters sprawled and twisted all over the page. I looked at the closing. It was just signed, "Charlie," and the date was May 15, 1864.

Dear Mrs. Wilson,

I reckon this is the hardest letter I've ever had to write, but I do because of Milton, who was like a son to me. I know you'll be receiving one of those black-bordered envelopes with its fancy condolences signed by President Lincoln, but I wanted you to hear a personal word about Milton.

Of course, he's dead or I wouldn't be writing to you. It's been three days since they said those nice things about him and read Scripture. I placed lilies on his grave. He told me about you, you know.

It happened like this: They never got to Red River on account of General Banks being defeated there while they were on the march. Since Banks had retreated, General Steele didn't think it was very smart to face the combined armies of Price and Smith, so they left to return to Little Rock on April 30. Price and Smith commenced to chase them and finally caught up at Jenkins Ferry on the Saline River. The stream was swollen and the swamp could not be gotten over anyhow, so they had to wait for pontoons to ferry them. Price and Smith attacked like savages. They were fresh from the victory at Red River, and there ain't nothing that makes a soldier fight more than winning—it's like throwing red meat to a wild dog. Well, Steele held them back and finally Price and Smith put their tails between their legs and took off.

During the fighting Milton was shot in the leg. I was with him while they removed the bullet. Things looked fine for a few days. Milton was the happiest I'd seen him, talking about being released because of his injury and going home. Then infection set in—surgical fever, they call it. When they removed those bandages, I knew what it was—gangrene. I'd seen it more times than a lot of doctors. There was one doctor who argued with the others, saying the maggots shouldn't be cleaned out of the wound. He said they cleaned out dead tissue and kept the infection down. But the other doctors wouldn't listen to such a thing. Since they was older and of a higher rank, their way won.

I told Milton that cutting off his leg was his only chance. I know. Wasn't I living proof of that? But Milton just shook his head. He'd hear none of it.

"A farmer can't earn a living with one leg," he said. "Martha needs a whole man. A boy doesn't need a pa everyone pities. I'd sooner die. Besides, how do I know I won't die, anyway, with it off? There ain't too many men like you with a wooden leg, Charlie,'' he said.

Every day his leg would look a little greener and the dark splotches got bigger and bigger. He wasn't in pain no more, though. Just had the chills and a fever.

I quit trying to persuade him to get his leg cut off. I could see from the color in the other parts of his body it was too late for that. Blood poisoning had already set in.

I sat by his side as much as my duties would allow. He never said bitter words, not even one. I'd heard plenty of men cussing God, in his same condition. He talked a lot about you and his son as if he'd see you any day. His last words were, ''Tell Martha I'll be home in May.'' I don't rightly know what he meant by that, but maybe you do. That was May 12th about 10:00 in the morning.

I can tell you, Mrs. Wilson, that a finer man than your Milton I never knew.

Charlie

Pa said his pa did go home that May—to his heavenly home. Was he waiting there for Martha with lilies in his arms? I liked to think so.

When Pa was five, his mother married Doctor Martin. They had a girl whom she named Lilly. Martha died before Lilly was grown.

I tied the letters to two sides of my waist again, and taking a handful of huckleberries to eat on the way home, left Orchard Pond.

CHAPTER 6

Fall, 1896

IT HAD BEEN A SAD SUMMER SO FAR and I aimed to
make up for it. Carl and Elsie and I played hide-and-
seek every chance we got. I let Lulu play even though
she was only four and kept giving her hiding spots
away. Baby Martin was giggling so much when I
picked him up I thought his belly button would pop
open. I didn't even mind the chiggers as much as I used
to, but Ma made us take baths in soda water every night
to get rid of them.

Being at Grandpa Martin's and reading those letters
seemed to make me grow up faster. I ran after the
geese which had frightened me the summer before.
After a good chase, I'd take a slow drink of buttermilk
from the tank Pa kept for the men working on the
railroad. If you held the milk in your mouth for a
while and then let it slide down, you could taste the

butter chunks. I wasn't even afraid when we had so much rain that the Nemaha River behind our house covered the road. I figured I'd just grab a board if the house was flooded and float around in the river like those big old catfish till somebody rescued me.

I couldn't wait for school to start. Clare lived too far away for me to see her much in the summer. And Nanny Allen, the teacher, had gone out east to see her folks. Pa would soon take us all into town to get new clothes and shoes.

Everything was going just fine until Ma said, "We're going to move to Oklahoma."

"Oklahoma? Where's that?" Carl asked.

I ran to look at my map. It was just the next state over, but somehow it seemed as far away as Switzerland. I remember when I was just three listening to Ma pray for Pa in Oklahoma when we lived in Kansas.

Ma and I were out picking up the peaches on the ground in the orchard. Ma would examine them real good, turning them over and over for brown spots. She put the ones with brown spots in a basket for us and the other ones we'd take to town and sell. Ma turned her lapel watch upside down to look at the time.

"One o'clock—the race is about to begin. Let's pray to the Good Man for Pa."

Ma lifted up her head (she always said you should pray looking up outdoors since God's heavens were prettier than the ground—less'n of course it was raining real hard). "*Please take care of Pa. Help him to get a good piece of land and—if we're not supposed to move—I pray that he'll come home empty-handed.*"

Well, good thing Ma put in that last part, because it turned out that was exactly what happened. All Pa's brothers got land next to each other along a creek, but Pa, he never found any that suited him—until years later. Pa's account of the land rush turned out to be Carl's favorite story; so we all got to know it by heart.

Pa would say, "Well, we lined up, neck to neck on our horses—horses as far as you could see. I say maybe four or five hundred."

Carl would just whistle and echo, "Four or five hundred!"

"Somebody fired a gun," Pa continued, "and we all raced to the creek—that was the best land. Why, I saw men forcing other men off their claim with a gun after they had already put down their stakes. But I didn't aim to stop and settle no disputes, no, sir, not with a man with a gun. Now actually some of these men had sneaked out to stake a claim even before the race began. Those 'sooners' should have been forced off, but who was to know who was a sooner and who wasn't? Yep, this Oklahoma Land Rush of 1889 will be famous one day. You'll see, my boy!"

"Golly! Wish I could've been there!" Carl would say, slapping his thigh.

We set out for Oklahoma on September 3, 1896. I remember the date exactly because it was the opening day of school. I tried to be cheerful for the younger ones' sake but, everytime I thought of Clare sitting at her double desk without me, I wanted to cry. We took three wagons between our family and the neighbor Gilkisons—one for each family and one for supplies. We took Prince, Dad's horse, and the Gilkisons took their cow Molly. Before we left Salem we filled our gunny sacks with apples—Maiden-blush, Golden Pippins, and Ben Davis. We also filled our pockets with apples and black walnuts. Lulu wanted to take all walnuts because she said she liked them much more than apples.

"All right, Lulu," Carl said. "But don't be beggin' us for apples. And don't be pickin' up no road apples from Prince, either."

We all burst out giggling but Lulu just kept asking over and over, "What's road apples, Carl?"

Inside our wagon we had our beds and a stove. We mostly walked and only rode when we got too tired. I liked seeing new country and I hoped I'd see some mountains just popping up out of the prairie—all white and fir-treed. I had checked my world map and didn't find any. But I thought since it was an old map maybe there were some that had sprung up since then.

The only white I ever saw wasn't snow but cottonwood trees. They weren't much good for anything, but when we got bored we'd sneak some of Ma's molasses and rub it on our faces and stick the cotton on to make beards and moustaches. Carl got one of his moustaches to curl way up on the corners by rolling it in his hands and coating it with tree sap to make it stiff. He chased after Amanda Gilkison with it, tickling her on the cheeks. She'd pretend to run as hard as she could and just when Carl was about to give up, she'd slow down so he could catch her. I had her all figured out. She had run the three-mile race at school. Carl could never catch her if she really tried.

The most fun was at night when we'd set up camp.

We camped along the Cimarron River so we'd have plenty of water. Smelling the sweet potatoes boiling over the fire and hearing the bacon crackle would make us so hungry we'd be holding our plates a half hour before it was ready. After dinner Mr. Gilkison would take out his harmonica and we'd have some singing. "Oh, Suzanna" was my favorite. We'd change the words from "I'm bound for Alabama" to "I'm bound for Oklahoma."

And then there were the stories. My favorite was how Great-Grandpa Isaac and Great-Grandma Sarah met. Whenever Pa told it, Amanda would edge a little closer to Carl. Then Carl would edge a little further away until Lulu or Elsie would yell, "Ouch!" Which meant he had stuck his elbow in their side or sat on one of their legs.

But I wasn't really thinking so much of Carl and Amanda when I was sitting around the campfire. I was thinking about Isaac and Sarah. Why, sometimes I'd think about it so much that I would hear the sound of the horses' hoofs as someone came running into our camp to marry me.

I saw in my mind those long wagon trains twisting over the plains like chain-linked fences going in opposite directions. Then I thought about that night where the two trains criss-crossed, making an X. I know it was real starry out, with a full yellow-orange moon looking as big as a hill. Maybe Isaac spied her at the square dance. I guess she was real pretty. Maybe he asked her to go for a walk away from the wagons. They wouldn't have gone too far, though, since there were a lot more Indians around back then. I bet she thought she'd never see him again, but he just couldn't get her out of his mind.

When he decided to turn around and try to catch her wagon train, they were already four days apart. He must have ridden hard to catch her. I'm sure he didn't waste much time asking her to marry him since he had to take her and catch the other train. I don't think Ma and Pa would ever let me ride off and marry some stranger who was gonna take me a thousand miles from home. And she couldn't take nothing with her, going on horseback, except maybe one dress.

Ma said, "She must have really been 'stricken' with love. But I guess it worked out, otherwise we all wouldn't be here." I wondered how long it would take me to know my "true love." I heard that phrase "true love" from a book called *Sleeping Beauty* that Nanny Allen had read to us in school.

Thinking about Isaac and Sarah were my "nighttime" dreams. During the day I still thought a lot about nursing people. I had it all worked out in my mind. I'd live in a big house with my rich husband and children and I'd have five bedrooms. Maybe I wouldn't do much nursing till my children were grown. I'd have two "patients" in each room, unless it was a mother with a new baby. The only thing I didn't have worked out was the price. Ma said that didn't matter anyway since you took what they gave you, which sometimes was nothing. Ma always used her nursing money for Christmas.

She had delivered over one hundred babies, and she kept a list of their names in a paper in her Bible. No matter how tired she was when she came home, she always entered the baby's name and date in her Bible right away.

One night when we were just sitting around the fire, I heard a rider come up. I was having my usual Isaac and Sarah thoughts and for a minute I said to myself, "He's coming for me," but it was Ma the rider wanted. His wife was having a baby, and he had seen the light from the fire. He was on his way to a neighbor's who lived five miles further on down, but thought he'd see if anyone could help him here. Pa was a little worried about letting Ma go with a stranger, but Ma just said, "Oh, hush, Milt! I'll be all right."

Ma still hadn't come home at breakfast the next day. Pa kept pulling out his pocket watch and looking toward the east where she had gone off with the rider. Pa said, "If she's not here by noon I'll start out." I didn't want Pa to leave, too, so I started getting real worried.

Just a little before noon we saw the rider and Ma coming. He was saying something to Pa and giving Ma a blanket. It wasn't like any blanket I had ever seen before. It had patterns in it like V's and bright colors—red, blue, yellow. Ma didn't go to her Bible right away to write down the baby's name. Instead, she climbed inside the wagon and lay on the bed. I was dying to hear all about it, especially since Pa said it was an Indian blanket, but I knew Ma needed sleep.

Pa made dinner that night and said no one was to wake Ma. We all had to sleep outside instead of in the wagon. Mrs. Gilkison took baby Martin in their wagon to sleep. When he carried her breakfast the next morning, I knew something was wrong. Pa still wouldn't let any of us in.

"Ma's sick, ain't she, Pa?" Carl asked.

Elsie and Lulu and me came running over wanting to hear. "Yep, she is. We don't know what's wrong with her."

Pa couldn't let us go to see Ma. When we asked why we couldn't, he always mumbled something about it being "contagious." Carl said, "That means ya can catch it." Knowing Ma was lying in the wagon sick and all made the rest of the trip not so fun.

Pa said, putting his hand on my shoulder, "Well, Ina, you'll have to be the mother for a while." Neither he nor I realized then just how long "a while" would mean. Since Pa was up driving the wagon or leading the horses, it was up to me to take care of baby Martin. It made me feel all grown up to be feeding and burping him just like Ma did.

Pa said we'd have to be careful crossing the Cimarron River because of the current. He made a rope for Carl and me to hang on to behind the wagon. The Gilkisons took in Elsie, Lulu, and Martin. I wasn't scared. The trip was getting awful tiresome, and the water was mighty warm. Pa took Prince over before us. Prince didn't want to go in. Pa said later that animals have "pre-monition" about things like that. Pa crossed a little to the right of us with Prince. He and Prince were getting a little behind us 'cause Prince kept balking and trying to turn around. It wasn't long before we heard Pa shout, "Quicksand!" Carl started to turn around but Pa yelled, "Go on! Go on!"

I glanced back at Pa. The water that had been up to his knees was up to his waist now. Prince was rearing his head up, trying to stay above the water. I started to cry. I was afraid to look any more—afraid I might see Pa's black hat floating on top of the water. When we got to the wagon on the bank, there was Pa behind us, but not Prince. We circled around him—Lulu, Elsie, Carl, and I still tied to each other by the rope around our waists. We got all tangled up and Pa said, "I feel like a calf roped and tied, ready for the branding." Mrs. Gilkison had to come with a knife to undo us. She said it was a wonder we didn't get cut the way we were a'giggling and wouldn't hold still.

After losing Prince and with Ma sick, we were glad to hear that the trip was almost over. I was looking forward to seeing Uncle Jim and all my cousins, but mostly I was looking forward to his house. I imagined it big with white pillars. After three weeks of hard ground, tonight I'd sleep on a featherbed. I think Carl and I were the first to see Uncle Jim's place. Pa called out and said, "There it is on the river!" All I could see was a shed. I thought that must be where they keep the animals. I kept looking for the big white house Pa must be pointing to, but I couldn't see it. As we got closer I kept thinking the house must be awfully far from the shed. I guess I didn't believe it till we got up to the door of the shed and Uncle Jim came out and hugged Pa.

That night I slept on my coat laid over the floor boards, staring at the grass sticking out of the mud bricks on the wall.

Uncle Jim's house was disappointing, but there were a couple of things to look forward to in November. The first of November we were going to the "old Brown place" where Grandpa and Grandma Hessor lived in Ingalls. Grandpa was going to be ordained and we were going to have a reunion too. Later on in November we were going to a political rally for McKinley.

November first was sunny and bright. We drove the fifteen miles to Grandpa and Grandma's in Pa's newly-washed buggy. Since I was the most careful of the kids, Ma said I would hold the cake she was going to enter in the contest. I didn't mind holding it because it was my birthday cake. It was colored pink from the raspberries Ma had saved, with peppermint candy crushed on top from last Christmas. When nobody was lookin', I'd swipe a little frosting off the sides.

Carl was asking Pa why Grandpa wanted to be ordained when he was almost ready to die. Ma, overhearing, said, "Carl, hush."

But Pa said, "Well, he is sixty which does seem pretty old, but you're never too old to make your dream come true. He's worked all his life to be educated enough to preach."

"Why does he want to preach, Pa?"

"I think he's so happy with religion and God, he wants other people to be happy, too."

"Did you ever want to preach, Pa?"

"Yeah, I guess so. I guess I still would like to."

Pa's answer surprised me. I'd been dreaming again—just sort of half listening.

I never saw such a mess of people, with Ma nudging me and telling me, "Now don't forget your name." I counted over fifty people before I lost track.

We all squeezed into the Mt. Hope Church for the ordination. The preacher was young and good-looking, so I tried to listen. He was saying there was more to life than everyday living—planting, plowing, and picking, and that Grandpa always knew that and sought "higher things." "Even for you younguns whose life is just beginning (he seemed to point his finger right at me) there's things better than marrying and making money. Only knowing Jesus is going to make you happy." I began looking out the window thinking about Sam Hall's blond lock of hair that always brushed his forehead as he walked.

When he came to the place where Grandpa got up to be prayed over, I stole a peek at Pa. While the praying was going on, he had his hankie over his nose and a tear was just landing on the initial T. I had never seen Pa cry before. Was he crying because he wished he could be ordained? Or did God move him that much? I decided he was crying for the first reason. Somebody you can't even see couldn't make you get all emotional like that.

After church the menfolk talked about the upcoming election. I broke away from Pa to watch the cake judging. Ma's didn't win, but it sure tasted good. Carl was holding his stomach all the way home from eating so much of it.

Elsie and I couldn't wait to go to the rally with Pa. We didn't really know what a rally was but trips with Pa were fun.

The rally was in this great big tent. There was a band with red uniforms on and a lady singer, but the part Elsie and I liked best of all was the sixteen girls (we counted them twice so we could tell Ma) all dressed up in white and gold. They wore little white hats with gold tassels on their heads and shouted,

"Rare—rare—rix!
Bryan's in a fix!
McKinley's on top in 1896!"

After they filed off stage, McKinley came on. "There's the next president," Pa said. He looked real kind, I thought. I didn't understand much of what he said, but I thought the way the smile lines in the face were, that he'd make a kind Grandpa.

All the way home Elsie and I chanted,

"Rare—rare—rix!
Bryan's in a fix!
McKinley's on top in 1896."

We had lots to tell Ma.

CHAPTER 7

Winter, 1896

WINTER CAME EARLY THAT YEAR and winter, Pa
said, was no time to build a house. So here we were in
Oklahoma—Pa, Ma, Carl, Elsie, Lulu, Martin, and
myself in one room—and Uncle Jim, Aunt Flora, and
cousins, Mary, George, Estel, Adrianna, and Audrey
in another. That made fourteen according to my reck-
oning, and I sure wished I was back in Nebraska. To
top it all off, Ma still wasn't feeling well, which left
me as the oldest girl to kinda take over for our family.

"Don't worry, Inie," Pa said, squeezing my shoulder. "By May we'll be in our own house and things
will have settled down a bit. Why, the cotton will be
in the ground and the peanuts, and we'll be happier
than ever."

Well, I usually believed Pa, but I didn't see how I
could ever be happier here than in Nebraska.

78

Sure enough, it seemed like things just went from bad to worse. We even got lost going to Union Home School. Uncle Jim's oldest boy, George, said he could find the way in his sleep. We should have known he was just smarting off. He always acted like he knew everything. Pa said we must have wandered over a mile away from school. George kept whimpering, "The trees looked different last year." Since he was only eight, it was hard to fault him, especially with the trees standing so thick together. Anyhow the next day Pa went with us to school and tied a white rag around each tree. I was glad he did. I was terrified of getting trapped in the woods, especially at night. When Pa ran out of white rags, he used the red hankie in his pocket. That red hankie just about got us killed.

I always told Carl it was his horrible singing that made the bull charge. That old bull probably thought it was a mating call. We could have crept on by the fence real quiet-like but Carl, declaring that he "wasn't scared of any old bull," launched into another chorus of "Skip to My Lou" without even batting an eye. We heard some loud pounding and snorting and Elsie yelled, "Run!" The top fence rail suddenly was in splinters. I wasn't curious enough to wait around to see if the bull could ram the next rail and get out. I think we ran the last half-mile home without stopping. The next day Pa mapped out a new route for us.

That winter was extra cold. Grandma Showater, one of the black ladies living near us, said never in her life since she had come from Africa had it been colder this early. ''Those Cherokees must be starving to death, Inie, chile,'' she said to me.

Now, Carl liked to hear about the Indians, but not me. The only Indian I wanted to see was the wooden one on the porch at the grocery store. Pa had faithfully passed on all the scalping stories he had been told until I had decided to sleep with my hat on every night. I figured they'd have to take my hat off first and then I'd wake up and be able to run for it.

All us kids slept on the floor. Carl and George wanted to sleep near the door. The little kids thought they were brave, but I thought they were just plain dumb. Me, I picked the spot right under the window so I could get out quickest. No one ever told me Indians don't come through doors; they come in the windows.

Well, I wish I'd slept through it like the others, but I had just waked up from my closet nightmare to see a flash of leather strips pass over me. Above me, the second Indian was jumping over my head. They lifted the lid on the pork barrel and began filling a gunny sack. I grabbed my hat. Whew! It was still there! I hadn't been scalped. Should I cry out? What if Pa or Uncle Jim got hurt catching 'em? They didn't have any paint on their faces or even any feathers. They looked so skinny and pitiful—like those stray cats we always let go through our garbage in Nebraska. Well, I was debating what to do when they left. I stayed awake awhile longer wondering if they would come back. Then I heard some faint cries—''Puckachee-puchachee, way-pachook.'' I wondered if they were celebrating their first meal in days.

The next day I was really tempted to tell, especially when Aunt Flora said, "It sure seems like we been using a lot more pork lately." But I just turned my back and smiled. It was such a nice secret to keep to myself and privacy was scarce around that house.

I didn't think nothing could scare me more than the Indian raid but I was wrong. Those stories Uncle Jim told that winter were much worse. Maybe it was 'cause your imagination is always scarier than the real thing.

Uncle Jim had gotten quite a reputation for being a hunter around those parts. He was personally asked to join a posse headed by the two most famous lawmen of the west (George said), U.S. Deputy Marshall Heck Thomas and Bill Tilghman. They were working for Marshall Nix, who was working for the President. That made Uncle Jim famous, I reckoned.

Uncle Jim told us it had happened a month before we arrived. "It was August 25—and I'll never forget that night as long as I live," he said. "The moon was bright and full when they came knocking on my door." Uncle Jim made a motion toward the window with his arm. We all glanced up, hoping we wouldn't see a face pressed against the glass. Elsie moved closer to me in the dark. The only light in the room was way in the corner where Ma and Aunt Flora were knitting. They had already put the little ones to bed.

Ma said, "Now, you don't need to waste expensive oil for storytelling."

Some of us took to watching Uncle Jim's face and the shadows that played on it from the fire. Others

81

watched the wood turn from fire-hot red to charcoal gray before the story was through.

"Now, Flora looked out and said, 'It's that Heck Thomas and Bill Tilghman.' Poor Flora; she hated to see them coming for me. To tell you the truth, I never got over being scared myself. There was always that little knot like somebody was squeezing a sponge in my stomach when I fastened on my guns.

"Usually either Thomas or Tilghman came alone for me—not both of them—but that summer we were hunting Bill Doolin. I knew that they must have found him even before they said something.

"Now, there are some men I don't mind hurting—although it's never pleasant to rough up a man except if it's that low-down Red Dog, killing an old preacher just because he protested him stealing his horse. I reckon Bill Doolin thought him low-down, too, because that's what got Red Dog kicked out of the gang.

"Bill Doolin was a different sort of outlaw. He had let Bill Tilghman go free after he walked into Doolin's hideout on Deer Creek on the banks of the Cimarron (just a little ways from here)." We all shuddered. "This is why Bill Tilghman went all alone to take him when he heard he was in Arkansas last winter. He couldn't kill a man who had saved his life. Five thousand were waiting at the Guthrie station to see him come in, and I was one of them. He wasn't even handcuffed. I got a real good look at Bill, being how Tilghman had asked me to watch the jail for a few hours. But I'm glad I wasn't watching it when Doolin made his escape seven months later.

"It was all these thoughts that were going through my mind on the way to Lawson. I wondered why there were so many of us to take one man. Maybe they thought some of his gang was with him. Thomas caught up to me and explained, 'Rose's husband, Charles, has been our spy.' Now, the Rose story we'll save for another night. He said Bill had been visiting his wife and child and planned to leave the country. Now, this news didn't make me too happy. It was bad enough to be killing a man, but killing a man who had some decency and in front of his wife and child at that, sure made me sick. Bill Tilghman must have been thinking the same thoughts, 'cause he said, 'The law's the law.' I was to hear him say that many times before the night was over. I know he was hoping we'd be able to take him alive when Doolin saw how outnumbered he was.

"We left our horses a good half mile away and walked in on foot. It didn't seem fitting to stalk a reverend's house like this—Bill's wife, Ellen, was a preacher's daughter. Their yard had the smell of roses like ours in the back where we play hide-and-seek. I wished like anything that I was home doing just that with you kids.

"As we got closer, we could see a loaded wagon with food, a couple of trunks, and a blanket bed like we make for the baby when we go traveling. There was a chicken coop and even a plow. It looked to me like Doolin was done with his life of crime. Just looking at that wagon made me start to fog up. I guess I had secretly wished we would find them gone when we came. *That close to happiness*, I thought, but then

83

I felt guilty like I was somehow thwarting the cause of justice.

"We each found a place to hide, watching the wagon, holding our rifles. The night was hot; my hands were sweaty. A little while later a breeze came up. The cottonwoods rustled above our heads.

"It took awhile getting a baby ready, I knew from helping Flora. Then they came—handsome Bill first, all six feet of him, his arm was around her waist. She was holding his son. It was the first time I had seen her. Her hair was all pinned up, brown and wavy. It was easy to see why Bill risked his life to court her. I couldn't see the baby. He was all wrapped up. Bill was saying something to her kinda wavin' his gun as he talked. She looked scared and glad all at the same time, kinda like George looks before he goes down a steep hill on a sled. When they got to the wagon, he kissed her sort of long and slow as if they weren't in a hurry at all, and then kissed the baby, lifting him in his bed. Bill swung her up on the buckboard and handed her the reins.

"Just as he was walking toward the lead horse, Heck Thomas yelled, 'Hands up or I'll shoot!' But it was Doolin who shot first—then Heck. Doolin missed, being in the bright moonlight, while Heck didn't, being in the shadows. When he pulled Ellen off of him, her blue calico was red, as red as the roses framing the yard. The Reverend came out and picked up the baby, who seemed to know something since he was crying, 'Papa, Papa.'

"We put Doolin's body on a horse and took him to town to the funeral parlor.

"Bill Tilghman told me he had seen the pewter cup that said *Baby* on it packed in the wagon. Bill had delivered it to Ellen at Doolin's request when he arrested him. Bill started to weep at this and I did, too. I wasn't sure I wanted to be on a posse anymore. After that night I just didn't have the stomach for it."

We all sat silent for a while after Uncle Jim had finished the story. Elsie was sniffing, and I was holding back tears myself. Even Carl and George were quiet for once. This was one night I was glad to be crowded into bed with Elsie.

After hearing about Bill Doolin, nobody begged for stories for a long time. But the nights were long and the days boring in the winter, and pretty soon we all wanted to hear another one.

"Now, this one's about Cimarron Rose," Uncle Jim began. We had all heard her name in connection with the battle at Ingalls. Pa even let us stand on tiptoe to look over the doors of the Trilby Saloon to see the bullet holes in the walls. "September 1, 1893, Heck Thomas came to get me for the first time. He heard I was a crack shot at hunting. We had just been back from Nebraska for ten months. Heck said they needed every available man because he heard the whole Doolin gang was gonna be in Ingalls, and they hoped to capture all of them at once. We rode in two covered wagons all scrunched up—only the drivers could be seen.

"The outlaws got wind that we were in town. We hid ourselves as best we could—shooting as we saw them sneak toward the livery stable to try and get their horses. Bullets were coming fast. The street was deserted. We had seen Deputy Tom Houston fall already, but didn't know if he was dead or alive. Bitter Creek Newcomb had been shot and Bill Doolin, but they both made it to the stable and there she was, running with her skirts and petticoat ruffles swishing, carrying a rifle on one hip and ammunition on the other. We learned later her name was Rose Dunn, one of 'Mrs. Pierce's girls' and Bitter Creek's lover. She had lowered his gun down on sheet-rags from the back window and then got down herself. She had been Bill Doolin's sweetheart first. Deputy Rick Speed lay behind a dead horse with Lafe Shadley. We saw him go down—hit between the eyes. We learned later it was Doolin's shot that done it.

"Rose and Bitter Creek escaped unbeknownst to us. Bitter Creek fell off his saddle, weak from the loss of blood. Deputy Shadley saw him fall at the same time Bill Dalton rode back to look for Bitter Creek. Shadley and Dalton shot at once. Shadley missed but Dalton didn't. Since Arkansas Tom was still shooting at us from Mrs. Pierce's Hotel, we couldn't pursue the outlaws. We decided to dynamite him out when Mary Pierce came out and said she'd get him to give up.

"He came out—just a kid. His capture had cost us three deputies. It wasn't worth it." Uncle Jim paused, with a look that was both sad and hard at the same time.

The boys asked more questions about the battle, but we girls were interested in Cimarron Rose. So Uncle Jim continued.

"Well, when Bitter Creek died, Rose married a blacksmith, Charles Noble. She had been only fifteen at the time of the battle. It was this Noble fellow, you remember, that told Heck when Doolin was visiting his wife, which led to his death. They said she was the prettiest thing in the territory. I didn't get a good look at her but her petticoats sure were fancy—not as fancy as your Ma's, though.'' He winked in Aunt Flora's direction.

I thought a lot about Rose and wondered how she could love an outlaw. Ma says the Good Man sees good in everyone, so maybe Rose saw something in him. I wondered if I could ever love a man enough to risk my life for him. I hoped I could, but I also hoped I wouldn't have to.

We were all glad to see spring come. Lulu noticed the buds on the trees first. She kept pointing to them and saying, ''Bugs, bugs.'' Elsie figured out what she meant.

School always let out early so the kids could help plant. Pa said they'd need all of us this year. Carl and George were begging to be able to handle the axes, but Pa and Uncle Jim wouldn't let them. Swinging that ax into dirt clods that were as hard as stone made Pa's hands leathery and lumpy. Ma called the lumps *callouses*. When the soil was soft we wet it down with buckets and planted the corn and peanuts. The mud kept your feet cool while your head was burning up. We planted potatoes, beets, and cotton, too. Of course, Ma and Aunt Flora had a big garden with every kind of vegetable you could think of. The alfalfa, oats, and millet were planted for the animals to eat. They were the most fun to plant. The seeds had to be "broadcast," or thrown as far as you could throw them. We'd have contests. Carl held the record, being a consistent ten-foot thrower.

Soon as we got everything in the ground, Pa said we were moving. We were going to work Aunt Lollie's old place. Well, at least all the planting was done. Uncle Bill had seen to that before he bought the new place. Although I'd miss Uncle Jim and all the kids, I'd be glad for some room. There were just too many people—including all the ghosts of those outlaws.

CHAPTER 8

Summer, 1897

ONCE IN A WHILE AUNT LOLLIE and Uncle Bill would come over and check on us, but usually we were pretty much alone, which suited me just fine. But there was one companion we always welcomed. Sabrina lived the next place over with her ma and pa. All her brothers and sisters had married, but because she was blind, she was left at home. We'd see her now and then at the berry patch. The fact is, Elsie and I enjoyed her so much we decided to run into Sabrina purposely from then on.

She'd hold onto me and Elsie as we walked real slow. The strawberry patch was quite a ways from the house. Sabrina knew we were getting close even before we saw the patch. "Umm—just smell 'em—must be ripe." Elsie and I looked at each other—how could she tell they were ripe just from the smell? As we got close Sabrina got real excited. "All right, all right, just set me down and hand me my bucket." She picked twice as fast as Elsie and me, and she couldn't even see. Once in a while she'd cock her head back and just hold it there, facing the sky. The first time I saw her do that, I came running over to say, "Stop! Don't look at the sun; you'll go blind." But then I remembered and caught myself just after the word, *stop*.

"My, the sun is glorious today, isn't it, Inie?" Sabrina said. Her legs were spread apart like a baby's in between the strawberry plants. "Listen! Hear that?" I didn't hear anything. "It's a mockingbird, I'm sure of it. At first I thought, *Robin,* then I thought, *No, must be a sparrow,* and then I was sure it was a canary. But, you know, a mockingbird can sound like all those and the song has been coming from the same tree all the time." *Now, how did she know that?* I wondered.

As summer wore on we made more trips with Sabrina. She could tell a blue morning glory from a pink one. She knew at which end of the clothespipe the yellow canary had built its nest. She could tell poisonous mushrooms from the tan-colored ones. They were all shaped like cones and porous like a sponge, except the poisonous ones were black on the underside. "Feel, Ina." She'd grab my finger. "There's two little holes in the poisonous ones."

I said, "Uh-huh," but I never did feel those holes. Sabrina was never wrong about mushrooms, and the way she carried on about wild cherries and gooseberries, I thought she'd never tasted them before. But it was the persimmons that she talked about the most.

"Just wait till the first frost! That's when they're the best, so purple and juicy. No fruit in heaven could be any better than that." Sabrina had us looking forward to the first frost like it was Christmas Day.

I wrote to Clare about Sabrina. I thought maybe Clare would know why she was so happy all the time when she couldn't even see. Me, I couldn't figure it out. I'd be madder than a hornet if it were me.

Some other people I couldn't figure out was the black family living on Aunt Lollie's place. They didn't have a penny. They didn't get to go to school. They had no shoes. Yet under their tent, which served as their church, they'd holler and sing as if they had just discovered gold.

They worked in the field with us, always singing, singing, singing, when my back was breaking, singing when little Martin was screaming as I dragged him behind me in a cotton sack, singing till the sun set, and singing the next day when it rose.

Oklahoma summers, as far as I was concerned, were nothing to sing about. The sand was so hot that, when we'd weed the beets, we had to wear pads on our knees. Some days it seemed like I'd look off and could almost see the trees in Nebraska, swaying next to the Nemaha River, but then they'd fade and there wouldn't be anything except mud and stubby green plants as far as I could see.

The only relief was stepping in that cool tub of water on the doorstep at the end of a day. "Inie really misses Nebraska," I overheard Pa say one night to Ma. But we hardly ever saw Pa. He was busy setting the water for irrigation and planting the cotton. We had three corn crops that summer, and it seemed we hardly got it planted before it was up again.

One night toward the end of summer, I was undressing for my Saturday night tub bath. This was gonna be extra special because I'd gotten a letter from Clare. I was saving it to read it later. Anyway, I had just settled in the tub when I heard Carl come in yelling, "Tornado! Tornado!" I jumped up and threw my dress on over my head. Sure enough, out the window was a swirling cloud with a tongue.

Pa was shouting, "Run to the cave! To the cave!" as he picked up Martin under one arm and Lulu under the other. Ma grabbed a loaf of bread. We crept back into the darkest part. We always kept cowhide spread on the floor in case we needed to spend the night there. Pa was telling us what he had seen. "Now, the white clouds mean wind, but the dark ones—that's hail. We're really in for it. Good thing it's late in the day because all the livestock are in the barn," he said.

I was afraid at any minute to hear the animals squeal and screech which could mean the barn had come down, but everything was quiet except for the steady pounding of the hail above us and my repeating the Twenty-third Psalm over and over in my mind.

The next day we moved out to inspect the damage. One wall of the house had been blown in, but since it was a storage room and things were packed tightly together, not much was scattered. Clare's letter was on the floor next to the tub, a little soggy but I could still make it out. She was answering my musings about Sabrina.

"You know, Inie, Sabrina does have eyes—she

92

sees and feels beauty we don't even know is there. As for not being bitter, maybe her life is so full of love there's no room left." Well, I knew what Clare was saying, but I still didn't understand. Sounded just like stuff a preacher would say. Why should Sabrina love God so much when she was blind? I guess I just felt Clare was on His side again, with me out the door.

Uncle Jim stopped by later to see how we were doing. "Anybody hurt?" Ma asked. She didn't care much for the reports of building repairs, but was always concerned about people.

"Yep, poor blind Sabrina. She's dead. Seems she was outside and her folks didn't call her in time. They found her under a fallen branch."

She probably wasn't even scared of the tornado, I thought. I pictured her out in the wind, hands in the air, like she did to feel the breeze. *And now she won't get to eat any persimmons.* The first frost didn't seem like much to look forward to any more.

CHAPTER 9

Fall, 1900

RIGHT AFTER HARVEST WAS ALL packed away, everything seemed to happen at once. Pa came yelling and throwing me up in the air, with his hat full of money. "Come on, Inie, we're going to town to buy you a birthday present and to buy that land."

Now, Pa, much to my embarrassment and concealed pride, had decided that when each of us girls turned twelve they were going to have a corset. So, after telling me what to buy and putting the money in my hand, he left me at the general store while he went to the bank. Two proud people returned home that day—me, with my corset, and Pa, with his lumber for the new house.

The house was all warm and comfy by the time Cora, the new baby, arrived. Pa and Carl were hoping for a boy, but they were as delighted as the rest of us when they saw those frizzy blonde curls popping up all over her head.

Once we got settled in our house, the days seemed to flow together, the bad times and the good, as swift as the thawing water in the Cimarron River—except for the summer of 1900.

I seem to remember every day preceding my fourteenth birthday. This was the magic year, the year that romance could begin, the year I could go to play parties. The summer seemed to drag. Ma let me cross off the days on the calendar but that didn't seem to help any.

Elsie and I amused ourselves by teasing Lulu. Ma stayed so busy keeping Cora from toddling into trouble, I don't suppose she knew half of what was going on. We'd set Lulu on Old Pet and give him a whack. He'd go thundering down the pasture with Lulu squealing and screaming and hanging onto his mane. When her face was turning the color of Ma's strawberry preserves, that was our signal to stop Pet. Lulu would be so mad she wouldn't talk to us the rest of the day, but then in about four days (as predictable as rain clouds), she'd say, "I think I'll give Old Pet another try," and we'd be off again.

And then there was Lulu's Kitty—with a capital *K* because that was his name. He wasn't really a kitty, just an old tomcat Lulu mothered. The sight of that cat in diapers would set Elsie and me to giggling till I thought my corset would bust plumb open. We were always hiding Kitty from Lulu—sometimes in the feeding manger or under the cover in Carl's bed. That upset Lulu but I'm not sure it upset Kitty. The way he looked when he was found made you feel awful sorry for him.

One day we went too far. Lulu was dawdling over her lunch as usual—stacking her peas on one side of her plate—when Elsie slipped out with Kitty under her blouse. I followed, chiefly to be a lookout. We were just heading for the barn when Lulu came running and shouting, "Oh, Inie, Elsie, have you seen Kitty?" We sure didn't want to get caught in the act. (Up to then, Lulu had had no proof that we were hiding Kitty. We'd told Ma that Kitty must have just climbed in those places himself.) Lulu was gaining on us and there was no place to go since it was an open field. So Elsie, in a panic, dropped him down the well.

We ran off, not even listening for the splash, and hid in the bushes. Lulu was about to go back to the house herself when she heard Kitty's "Meow." I guess that was one place we hid Kitty where he wanted to be found. Lulu took one look down the well to be sure and went screaming into the house. Ma came out a minute later with a rag tied to the end of a rope. She lowered it into the well and we heard her say, "Come on, Kitty, Kitty, Kitty, come on." We sure were surprised when Ma raised up that pitiful wet cat clinging to the rag. I know that time he was glad to see Lulu.

Ma really questioned us when Lulu said she had seen us running across the yard, but we played dumb and Elsie said, "I reckon that cat was just curious about that well. You know how cats are, Ma, and that Kitty is a particularly intelligent one." We gave a look at Lulu, hoping to throw her off our track. It worked. Her suspicion changed to pleasure at the compliment, but Elsie and I decided we'd better find some new fun before we really did get in trouble.

Carl and Martin were keeping busy that summer being Indian braves. Martin had just turned four and was out to prove he could do everything that ten-year-old Carl could do. They'd smear raspberries all over their face for paint and dip bird feathers in honey so they'd stick to their arms. "Indians don't wear feathers on their arms," Elsie would point out.

"Yeah, but Ma said we can't plaster honey in our hair," Carl would say, sticking a blue-jay feather on his elbow.

Elsie would laugh, and me, too, as they'd go running to "hunt buffalo."

We'd say, "Don't go running into any bees or bears, brave Injuns."

It was during one of those buffalo hunts (which were really rabbit hunts) that we almost lost Carl and Martin for good. Martin told us later they were hot on the trail of a long-eared fuzzy-tailed buffalo when they saw him heading for a hole under the tree. Carl thought a little jab with his bow was just what that buffalo needed to drive him out. The rabbit didn't come out, but something else did—a copperhead snake. Carl said it seemed like it got both Carl and Martin in one swing of its head as they both looked into the hole.

I said it sure was lucky that Pa was passing by on the way home to lunch. Ma said it wasn't luck at all. The "Good Man" arranged it so. When Pa brought those boys home, one flung over each shoulder, I just knew they were dead. Ma came out screaming. Pa yelled, "Copperhead," and dropped them on the bed.

Ma was fixing chicken for supper, and I said later *that* was lucky. They sure would have been dead if they had had to wait for Ma to kill and feather a chicken. Again, Ma said, "It wasn't luck, Inie. The Good Man works out everything. Like it says in the Good Book—all things work together for good to them who love God."

Pa held part of the fresh-killed, still-warm chicken on Martin, while Ma held some on Carl. It didn't seem lucky to me that the Indian braves didn't have any shirts on, but Pa said a bite on the shoulder was better than the neck. I wanted to stay, but when the green pus came out on the cloth wrapped around the chicken, I thought I was gonna be sick. Elsie didn't look. Her face was turned toward the corner, her mouth mumbling prayers, her eyes shut. Lulu was right next to her, moving her mouth, but I'm sure her prayers were just gibberish. I took baby Cora and left since I wasn't being of much use.

About three hours later, Martin and Carl moaned, and the color began coming back in their faces around the raspberry "paint."

After that day Pa took Carl and Martin with him into the fields. He also took them into town and got them cowboy hats. I guess he figured being cowboys wasn't nearly as dangerous as being Indian braves.

CHAPTER 10

Fall, 1900

I WAS GLAD TO FEEL THE nip in the air. That meant my birthday was coming. And that meant play parties. At play parties you could dress up, and boys would notice you.

I'd been practicing rolling my hair on a rat for months. And I'd been told that Sam Hall had his eye on me. But I didn't have as much time for "primping," as Pa called it, as I'd have liked to. With Ma still not feeling well, the kids had to do a lot of the harvesting. We were sure glad to use Uncle Jim's cotton gin. It was a wonder—seeing those black seeds sucked right out of that cotton. I was so glad not to have to pick 'em one at a time. The thrasher machine that came around to all the neighbors took care of our hay.

The hard part were those 'taters. The ones we didn't

eat had to be cut in four pieces to plant in the spring. Sitting at that hard board, cutting cull potatoes for hours, would just about drive me crazy. Then I'd get anxious and hurry, almost always cutting my fingers when I did. I know my fingers were as cut up as Pa's face was sometimes on Sunday after shaving. But there was fun to be had—roasting peanuts in the oven, pulling taffy, visiting the chili stand when Pa took the cotton to town, and splashing in that big pond at the end of a hot day.

School seemed better this year. We went to Star Valley which was closer than Old Union and I marked off the days till my birthday. The day of my first play party finally arrived. On the way to the party I was pinching my cheeks, trying to get a blush in them like Mary always had, hoping Pa wouldn't notice. "Got an itch, Inie?"

"No, Pa, just checking my cheek curls."

"Now, don't be so vain, Inie. Boys are more interested in a girl that's fun to be with than a stuck-up beauty. You're mighty pretty, but don't put trust in your face."

Pa had never given me advice about boys before. I felt all grown up.

The first play party would be at Uncle Wes's house. Ma had surprised me with a new dress on my birthday. It was pink with a double ruffle on the bottom.

Little fat Edna was playing "Skip to My Lou" on the French harp when we got there. Uncle Wes was playing the fife, and Vannie was playing the mouth harp. All the cousins around my age were there. Rosa, John R., Myrtle, Ted, Milt, and Pete. Pete's girl,

Lucy Matthews, was there with her sister, Mamie Young.

As soon as Pa left, Sam Hall came over. He was dressed in a navy suit with a real silk shirt. You could tell his Pa had money. When Sam wasn't around, his sisters came over to tell me how much he had been talking about me. Sam stayed by my side right through the promenade. At the end of the party Sam squeezed my hand and said, "Sure enjoyed this evening, Inie."

As I was putting on my coat, I pinched my cheeks. I wanted Sam to remember me all glowing and pink like the color of my dress.

Since Sam was older than me, he had already been through Star Valley. That meant I only got to see him at the play parties which, in the winter, were only once a month. I couldn't wait till summer when they were every Saturday.

When the weather turned warm, the play parties were held outside. Kerosene lights were hung in the trees. Square dancing under the stars was lots more fun than in a house. Pa let Sam take me home now. Sometimes different boys would ask, but I'd say no. Freddie was every bit as good-looking as Sam but his folks were poor. I knew it was awful wrong of me to care about that, but I had my dreams—my dreams to see the Amazon, Mt. Kilimanjaro, and Texas. Freddie didn't even have a buggy. He would've had to walk me home. Not that Sam's buggy was so fine, but I knew, as sure as I knew my name, one day he'd have one with red velvet seats and a black leather canopy. Clem asked to take me home, too. It was easy to say no to him. He was always preaching at everybody.

One time, he even told me I shouldn't curl my hair. I was so mad at him my cheeks got pink naturally without my even pinching them. Sam was religious, but he was quiet about it, and strong, just like Pa. He wanted to be a preacher someday. I didn't think I'd make a very good preacher's wife, but then I could pretend to like it for Sam.

Sometimes on the way home, Sam would settle closer to me so our shoulders were touching. (Nobody except that floozy Tate Warner ever held hands or kissed before marriage. Why, she even waist-swang, letting boys put their arms all the way around her—but then she was "that kind of girl.")

Sam would say, "Inie, when you see all those stars so far away it just amazes me that the same God who made those cares about every step I take and loves me enough to die for me." I wasn't much interested in what Sam was saying when he talked religious like that, but I loved to hear the smooth sound of his voice against the rhythm of the horse's hoofs. I'd imagine his saying, "I love you, Inie" in that same smooth voice; but he didn't, and I knew he wouldn't, not till he was twenty, which would make me eighteen. That was when Sam would get his own house and farm. Sam wouldn't say, "I love you" without saying in the same breath, "I wanna marry you."

"Eighteen," I'd moan to Elsie. "Why, I'll be an old maid by then."

Elsie, now twelve and having outgrown her hatred of boys, would answer starry-eyed, "But a boy like Sam Hall—he's worth waiting for—any girl in Payne County would be glad to wait for him."

Everything was going well till Dick came along. Dick had been seen with Tate Warner more than once. We were all staying clear of him, yet at the same time we couldn't help admiring him. His hair was dark and his beard was so heavy he had a shadow even after he shaved, not like Sam's blond beard. Pa said teasingly Sam's beard was so thin that, if he put a little milk on it, the cat would lick it off.

Dick was so sure of himself that, even as I said no, he whisked me away. They were playing "Little Black Eyes, Get Along Home," but I didn't hear much of the music. Dick was saying things in my ear Sam wouldn't dare to say, like how much he would like to touch me and how my lips looked like ripe plums. He looked at me like I remember Uncle Bill looking at Aunt Lollie before they were married.

After the dance I ran over to where I hoped Sam would be waiting to take me home, but Dick followed. "I've got to see you. What about tomorrow down by the Orchard Pond? You know the place." I turned my head. Where was Sam? I climbed into the buggy. "*Au revoir*," Dick said as he grabbed my hand and kissed it.

Of course, I couldn't meet him. It was ridiculous. What if somebody saw me? What if Dick tried to kiss me? (Surely that was what he wanted.) What if he were just making a fool out of me and wouldn't show up? Yet I hadn't quite talked myself out of it. His looks and his swagger were the stuff dreams are made of, and my world had for years been made of dreams.

It was a hot July day. During church I kept turning it over and over in my mind. I finally decided there couldn't be any harm in just hiding in the bushes and seeing if he showed. Besides it would serve him right and even be kind of fun watching him wait around and then leave all disgusted-like.

So I waited, getting there early. I kept my church dress on because it was green and blue and I thought I'd blend right into the bushes. But one thing I hadn't figured on—Dick's getting there early, too. He came up behind me and put his hands over my eyes, saying, "Guess who?" like Carl used to do when we were kids. Only this time I felt all tingly inside and I smelled jasmine cologne. Dick whirled me around, "I knew you'd be here."

I protested, "I was planning to hide and watch you wait for me." I walked rapidly away.

Dick caught up and grabbed my arm, "Tell me you don't feel something when I touch you." My face got redder; he was right.

"There, you see. You do like me." I walked away faster.

"Come on, just sit down here by the pond with me. I won't touch you. Let's just talk."

Dick was true to his word; we did "just talk." He told me all about himself. He had been many places—New York, California. When the sun began moving west, I said, "I gotta go."

"What about next Sunday?" he asked.

"I'll think about it. If you don't tell anyone."

"You mean Sam Hall, don't you?"

Dick would watch me at the play parties but was careful not to be seen with me. I began to look forward to talks with Dick more than to the parties.

I talked myself out of feeling guilty about these Sunday meetings. After all, we were just friends. He hadn't touched me since he said he wouldn't. Yet he still looked at me that way. I'd lower my eyes or look away.

Toward the end of August, Dick said he was going away. He looked at me "that way," and I didn't look away. I thought for one silly moment, *I want to go with you.*

As if Dick could read my thoughts, he said, "Come with me, Inie," and grabbed my hand. That warm tingle again. "You know I love you." There—he had said it—on a hot August day, sitting in the cool grass, with his hand in mind—just how it ought to be.

"You don't want to stay here and wait for Sam for three more years." Dick had moved closer, his lips brushing the curls around my ear.

I jumped up, breaking the trance. "No, it's unheard of! Ma and Pa would never permit it."

"You could write them later on. They'd cool down. Especially when they see how rich you'd be. Meet me here next Sunday if you'll go with me."

All week long I thought about not even showing up. I wasn't mad at Dick because of his proposal. I was afraid that, if I saw him again and he asked me, I'd go.

When I approached Dick on Sunday, his face was tight, his eyes narrow. "No bag. You're not going."

"No, Dick, I can't."

"Then this is good-by." Dick drew me close. As we kissed I knew I had wanted that as much as he had. He held my head on his shoulder and begged "Inie, go with me. Go with me."

105

This was stronger magic than I had expected, but Sam's face came into my mind. Good Sam; steady Sam. I stepped back. Dick looked as if I had slapped him.

"Not good enough for you? Go marry your old Sam Hall. That is, if you live that long."

After his back was only a small dot across the fields, I sat down next to the pond where we had spent so many happy Sundays.

Now, all those Sundays were clouded like the tall grass I saw through my tears.

I wouldn't tell Sam about this ever; I wouldn't tell anyone. But I couldn't forget it. Remembering was like tasting Ma's watermelon relish. Sometimes it was sweet; sometimes, sour. It depended on which way your tongue swished it in your mouth.

CHAPTER 11

Summer, 1901

BEFORE SCHOOL STARTED WE HAD A little outing to Aunt Sadie's. She lived about fifty miles south of Stillwater in the Kickapoo country. I don't remember much about that trip now except that it was September 6, 1901. The headline on the newspaper that day read: "McKinley Shot." Pa and Ma were in tears, and I was awful sorry myself. I remembered McKinley's kind face from the rally. "What wicked men there are in the world," Ma said. We all included him in our prayers hoping he'd recover, but on September 14, he died.

I prayed for McKinley even after he died. Now that may seem strange to pray for somebody when he's dead, but I was praying that he was really dead. I was worried that they buried him too soon. I'd heard of that before and thought nothing could be worse. After the President's death, the closet in my nightmare would turn into a coffin. I'd be hammering my fists against the top and screaming, "I'm alive! I'm alive!" Then I'd wake up. After a few months this dream faded and my regular nightmare returned.

Uncle Jim was leaving his term as sheriff after successfully running twice. Aunt Flora was glad they'd be moving to Stillwater to start a store and do something "civilized."

Payne County, the hideout of the famous Doolin Gang, was still teaming with "lesser varmints," as Pa said. Aunt Flora was hoping Heck Thomas and Bill Tilghman wouldn't call any more, except, of course, for a social visit. Uncle Jim had stared death in the face many times, and Aunt Flora had stayed up many a night wondering if her husband would come home draped over the saddle instead of on it. I was glad for her they were getting out and glad Uncle Jim had become a hero around the county by serving the law.

As winter came, I settled into quilting. Everybody assumed it was for Sam. Certainly Sam's mother was pleased when I took up quilting. That meant I was serious about homemaking. Sam called every week now, even in the thick of winter. I worked hard on the quilting frame, so he could whistle and say, "Inie, that is beautiful." Grandma had given me a peace quilt; Ma was working on a diamond pattern. I chose the big star pattern. Just the name reminded me of summer play parties with the stars shining through the trees.

Once in a while I thought of Dick; I wondered where he was and what he was doing. Would I really have gotten to see all those exciting places with him? I knew Sam would probably live here all his life. Sam was so much like Pa—maybe that was why they got along so good.

This was my last year of school. Graduation was an exciting time. Ma had said the next time I'd have a dress so pretty would be my wedding day. Besides, all our relatives were coming, even the Hessers. Ma had baked cakes and ordered sweet nutmeats. The punch looked like the communion grape juice, and there were lots of my favorite cherry pies.

However, the Hessers didn't show up for graduation. We were a pretty disappointed group, all dressed up waiting at the house, staring at all that food. Well, it turned out Carl and Martin weren't staring when one of the pies came up missing and they looked like Indian braves again!

I decided to go out and sit in the hammock on the front lawn. The yellow canaries were singing as I swung, the breeze stirring the ruffles on my dress. I was thinking of Sam, then Dick, then Sam. I had a strange sense of anticipation. I pinched my cheeks. The grass waved slightly; watching it, I almost felt hypnotized. Maybe that was why I didn't hear anybody coming.

I looked up into his face; then jumped up and gasped.

"I didn't mean to scare you," he said.

"You didn't." That was the truth. It wasn't the suddenness of his approach that scared me. It was his appearance—he was the man in the Sears catalog, the man I had dreamed about so long ago; the very man with blue eyes like the Nemaha River. His light-blond hair, just like in my visions, was parted on the right and one big wave went up toward the back of his head.

I must have looked shocked. "My name's Porter," he said. "Porter Baker. I came up with the Hessers. We sure hated to be late, but the cows got loose, and it took awhile to get them in."

I was glad to walk in the house and be with the others. I needed time to think, to look at him from a distance, to pinch myself to make sure I was awake.

After everyone had gone I heard Ma and Pa talking about Porter. It seems he had grown up with the Hessers in Nebraska. "Had a sorrowful life, Grandma told me," Ma was saying. "Seems his first wife, Tibby, was a cripple, but a real pretty girl. She died of a cold while he was away getting a homestead. Had a child die, too."

Pa was shaking his head. "A sad blow for a man. Yet he don't seem bitter."

Married before, I thought to myself. I was disappointed, almost jealous, of this beautiful lame girl that had captured his heart. Yet he had known love and sorrow, and that made him all the more desirable and mysterious. *How old is he?* I wondered. As if Ma heard my thoughts from the next room, she said, "Don't look as old as twenty-six, does he?"

A man of twenty-six! Why, he'd never be interested in a girl of fifteen. But then why should I care? I had Sam, handsome, kind Sam. Yet he wasn't dream-stuff like Dick or Sears-Catalog material like Porter.

The Hessers and Porter seemed to come up often that summer. I hoped it was on account of me, yet

110

Porter spoke to me so little and was never alone with me. I often wondered what it would be like to touch him—to kiss him. But I knew if he ever was interested in me, I wouldn't let him till marriage. I'd take no chances of losing him.

One Saturday the Hesser boys and Porter showed up at a play party at Uncle Wes's house. Porter asked me to dance. Since the number was "Picking up Pawpaws," it seemed natural to talk about summer fruit and wading in the pond. He was easy to talk to like Dick, yet reserved like Sam.

Sam asked me about him on the way home. "Oh, him? He's just a friend of the Hesser boys." I didn't dare let my dreams run away with me. *Could he be interested in me?*

Then in the fall he came, his gray hat with the black suede ribbon in his hand, asking Pa if he could come calling on me. He had his own buggy—with red velvet cushions and a black leather canopy. I hoped if Pa said no, he'd at least let me have a ride in the buggy. That buggy looked as fine to me as Cinderella's coach must have looked to her.

Pa said yes, and so it was settled. The hard part was telling Sam. No respectable girl had two callers, since Saturday night was the only calling night. I didn't want to hurt Sam, and I didn't want to hurt myself by losing Sam. What if Porter was a poor risk? Other than his being a friend of the Hessers, I knew little about him. But I couldn't tell Porter about Sam. He might not ask to call again. If Porter didn't work out, maybe Sam would wait. Sam was a mere boy compared to Porter. I'd pinch myself to see if I was dreaming. How

111

could it be that Porter looked exactly like the man in my dreams? It was years before I'd find out.

I sent word through Sam's sister that I wanted to meet him down by the Orchard Pond. Sam came walking fast, holding his hat with one hand and wiping the sweat off his brow with his red hankie in the other. He was happy and held my hand as we sat down. "Inie, you look so pretty today."

"Thank you, Sam." Sam didn't usually say things like that. It made it all the harder to say what I had to.

"Sam, you know Porter, the man at my graduation party?"

"Sure, a nice fellow. You gonna watch his kids for a while? Now, you know I'll miss you, Inie, but if that's what you want to do, it's O.K. with me."

"No, Sam, that's not it." I drew my hand away. "He wants to court me."

"But he's too old, Inie. Your Pa would never let him. Do you want me to tell him to leave you alone?" Sam stood up and clenched his fists.

"No, Sam. Sit down please. Sam, I want him to call."

Sam looked puzzled and then hurt. "Inie, I'll ask Pa if we can be married right away—before your sixteenth birthday. We'll make it—we have some extra rooms in the house and—"

"No, Sam," I stopped him, "I have to see Porter. I have to find out if he's the one."

Sam stood up, his face contorted, and said, "Well, I won't wait, Inie. I won't." Sam walked away as fast as he had come. He never looked back as Dick had, hoping to persuade me with his mournful eyes. Suddenly I remembered Dick. This was Orchard Pond, the same place I had met Dick. I sat down and across my mind swaggered Dick and last summer's Sundays. And then came Sam, swinging me under the stars at play parties. The long grass blurred in front of me. Was this the place for good-bys? It seemed as if I saw another person walking away from this place today— her berry pail in her hand, skipping and laughing, ribbons waving in her hair. It was me. I wasn't sure growing into dreams was as fun as dreaming them.

CHAPTER 12

Fall, 1902

I NEVER FORGOT SAM, and I guess he never forgot me because he didn't take up with another girl like he had threatened to do. I thought about him mostly with pity as his sisters said he was really pining for me. But I never saw him at any play parties.

Porter was nice and polite to my parents, though he never won them completely over like Sam had. I think it was mostly his age. But at the time, their reservations didn't bother me. I was living my dream, and I didn't even notice if my feet were on the ground—I was always looking up at Porter. He wasn't like any of the other boys I knew, except in the areas I admired most—he was suave and sophisticated like Dick, with dreams of far away places, yet he was practical and kind like Sam. This was the source of enchantment for me.

Porter never took liberties. The only time we touched was when I fell asleep on his shoulder on the way home from a play party.

On Friday nights we went to literary society meetings. I was the youngest person there. We heard distinguished lectures on politics, literature, and poetry. The poetry readings were my favorite. I tried to concentrate on the others, especially the political ones, so I could discuss them with Porter. But they were just like most sermons to me—big words and hard to follow.

I think that fall the leaves were the prettiest I'd ever seen. Aunt Flora said, "It's always that way when you're in love." The red leaves seemed the reddest; the yellow, the brightest. Usually I was sad when they were all off the trees—but not this year. I was looking forward to buggy rides, with Porter, snuggled all cozy under the canopy, the blanket pulled over our legs, watching the snow come down.

My sixteenth birthday was approaching, too. Sixteen sounded a whole lot older than fifteen. "Old enough to be engaged," Elsie said. I agreed with her. I wanted Porter to ask me, really I did, but I was afraid if he did, Pa would think we were rushing things. When my birthday passed I began worrying that he wasn't interested enough to marry me and that he was just passing time, but common sense (and Elsie) told me that a man his age wouldn't be courting unless he were serious.

At Christmas Porter said, "Inie, I've got a surprise for you." I knew he was going to ask me then. I had worn my graduation dress, with a red silk sash, and

115

stationed myself in the middle of the couch so I could display the ruffles on my dress on both sides. (I didn't think Porter would be sitting anyway, but kneeling, of course.)

Porter's surprise turned out to be a present. It was wrapped all in gold paper—the shiniest paper I've ever seen. I tried not to be disappointed and I almost forgot that I was expecting a proposal when I saw how pretty the opera shawl was. "Oh, Porter!" I said, running my hands over its blue and white threads, "I've never had anything like this!"

"It goes with your blue eyes." Porter left his hand on my shoulder after he had draped the shawl over me. Maybe it was Christmas, or the blue shawl, or just wanting to be proposed to so badly, but I turned my face toward Porter to within an inch of his lips. Porter was embarrassed and stood up quickly. Kissing was something only married people did—maybe engaged people, if they didn't tell anyone.

I was disappointed, but I knew Porter was right. I couldn't figure out why he was waiting so long. He certainly was old enough and now I was, too. Was he judging my character? My cooking? My quilting?

Just when I was feeling like we'd be courting forever, it happened. It was during the first big thaw. I was thinking how I'd like to get out in the sun and warm my bones when Porter dropped in and asked if I'd like to go for a buggy ride. Since I hadn't expected him, I just had on my gray housedress. On the way out the door, I grabbed my opera shawl. Porter had a shine in his eyes. *Must be spring*, I thought, but it wasn't.

He stopped the buggy down by the Orchard Pond. It

116

put a sort of sadness in the day, and I wished he'd stopped somewhere else, but then it did look different than in the summer, and I wasn't saying good-by to anyone this time.

Porter said, "Isn't this a pretty spot? And isn't this a pretty girl?" He grabbed my hand as he spoke, "Inie, you'd be a good wife and a good mother. I want you to marry me. Will you?" Even though I had rehearsed my answer a million times, I couldn't speak. I just looked at his hand on mine and then up at his eyes. Yes! They were as blue as the color of the Nemaha River in springtime.

"Yes, Porter."

"We'll be happy; you'll see. I'll take you all those places you've always wanted to see. And I promise you, we'll be rich." I wondered how anyone could promise that, but I guess I didn't know then how determined Porter was.

When Porter put his arm around me, I was wishing I had rolled up my hair. I felt all tingly like with Dick, but also safe like with Sam. The thought of kissing crossed my mind, but I reasoned that Porter would wait till marriage, and I was right. We did do a lot of hand-holding that spring and summer though.

The first summer play party was at Porter's place. He had moved closer and was farming with a neighbor. The party was to announce our engagement. Porter had taken me into town and, pressing some money into my hand, he said, "See that dress shop?" It was The Gay Paree. I looked down at the money in my hand.

"There's enough money," he said. "Don't worry.

Buy the best dress there is, and some shoes—some of those white satin slippers." I had never had so much to spend before—fifteen dollars! I chose a pink lace with little red hearts. "Hand embroidered," the sales lady said. The white slippers had hearts on them, too.

When Porter came to get me, I had one request, "Can we drive through town?"

"Anything you want. It's your party."

I had guessed right. Priscilla Newsbickle was just coming out of her house then for her evening walk. I put my hand on Porter's arm, "Slow down a bit, Porter," I said, and in the same breath, I shouted, "Hello, Priscilla!" I made sure both my feet were on the right side of the buggy and pulled my dress up a little so she'd have a clear view of my slippers. I hoped we had gone slow enough so she could see the red velvet seats.

"A friend of yours, Inie?"

"I've known her since grade school." So all my dreams were coming true, even this one. But I wasn't as happy as I thought I'd be. In fact, I felt rather foolish and was glad when Porter changed the subject.

Porter's house and yard had more swinging lanterns than I've ever seen. Yards and yards of pink ribbon were strung from tree to tree. "It's your favorite color, isn't it?" he asked. I was so overcome, I didn't know what to say, I was thinking how much money this had all cost. "Now if you're worrying about the money, don't. We're gonna have lots of it some day." Porter swung me down from the wagon.

The food table had pink-frosted cookies, nuts, and chocolate candies. When I arrived my cousins and friends rushed up with congratulations so the announcement was sort of anti-climactic—everyone knew already. Sam's sister Evelyn congratulated me later. "I am happy for you, Inie. Don't think these tears mean a thing." She didn't have to explain. I knew the tears were for Sam. I wished Sam would find a girl. If he had I would have felt so much better about the engagement.

Porter was sort of a Prince Charming to the other girls. Coming in from the outside like he had, and being older gave him an air of mystery. These facts plus his natural good looks and polite manners made him a desirable bachelor. I was glad for the engagement because some of the girls had started to flirt with him. And Porter, being such a gentleman, was kind to them all. Sometimes I actually thought he enjoyed their attentions, but I dismissed this thought as foolishness. He was just being polite. All the same I was glad he was no longer eligible.

That night I felt so special. When time for the announcement came, Porter had another surprise for me, "The wedding date is August 6. You're all invited." Amid cheers and shouts of "Hurrah!", I grabbed Porter's hand and whispered, "That's Ma and Pa's twentieth anniversary. They'll be so pleased, Porter."

"I know," Porter said with a slight smile.

CHAPTER 13

Summer, 1903

THE SUMMER WAS PASSING QUICKLY. I couldn't decide if I wanted it to or not. I was looking forward to August 6, but then the expectation and the "promise-time," as Ma called engagement, was such fun.

As I look back it seems like we had lots of time together, but I know we probably didn't because Porter had just bought our new place. That was another wonderful surprise—it was only a mile-and-a-half from Pa and Ma's place. Porter was over there plowing and planting. I wanted to help, but Ma said, "Now, he's got Pa and the neighbors to help him. Our job is the house." We made yellow-checked curtains for the windows and flowered calico for the bedroom. We scrubbed those floor boards till I thought the grain in the wood would be worn away.

When it was too late to work and Porter had enough

energy to drive over, we'd go out walking. He'd try to finish his work early so we could watch the sunsets. With the sky lit up and Porter's hand in mine, sometimes I thought I had died and gone to heaven. On Sunday afternoons we'd just sit and swing in the hammock and made plans for the future. When we weren't planning, we were dreaming silently. Sometimes we'd go flower-picking. Poppies were fair game since Ma had a slew of them. "Always pick them slowly, never jerky," Porter had told me, "that's the secret of getting all the petals to stay on." I wasn't afraid of the darkness any more. As if in anticipation of never being alone again, I quit having my closet nightmares.

The summer was hot, but I didn't mind. In between scrubbings and sunsets, we went to play parties and box socials, where Uncle Van would auction off picnic lunches the girls had packed. Van had just married Augusta the winter before. There was some lively competition—even for mine—which surprised me. Porter said, "You'd think those fellows would realize we'll be married in less than a month."

"Maybe they think they can turn my head with those high bids," I teased.

"High bids? I'll show you high bids! Ten dollars!" Porter shouted. There was silence in the room. The highest bid ever before had been $2.50, which everyone thought outrageous. After the engagement party Porter got the reputation of being a big spender. They were shocked but not surprised.

I kept looking for Sam Hall at these functions. It was funny that I hadn't run into him in all these months. The town just wasn't that big. Since decent girls were supposed to keep their eyes downward when they walked (only brazen girls stared a man right in the face), Sam could have seen me without my seeing him. But I saw him first—on August 4, just two days before the wedding.

He was down by the Orchard Pond, a place I came to now and then to get away for a bit from all the flurry of the wedding preparations. I got a chance to look at him before he saw me. Blond and blue-eyed—just the same—except looking a little older. *A fine husband he'll make,* I thought. *In a little over a year he would have been mine—if Porter hadn't come along.* Sam saw me and turned to go. "Sam, Sam." As I called he turned around. He was twirling his hat around in his hand real slow.

"Been working hard, Sam?"

"Yep."

"I'm getting married, Sam." *What a dumb thing to say,* I thought. He already knew. Did I want him to protest?

"I know. Evelyn told me. Staying 'round here?"

"Yep. Cottons' place, just west of here."

"Uh-huh," Sam turned to leave.

I touched his sleeve. "Sam, I do miss . . . your friendship."

Sam looked at me with the most painful expression I've ever seen. Then I knew why Sam hadn't found himself another girl. I wanted to say, "Sam, you'll be happy. You'll find a girl better than me. She'll love you. You'll have a family." Instead I lowered my eyes and walked away—slowly. I didn't think much about Sam for a long time after that.

My wedding dress was the latest fashion—Porter saw to that. It had a high neckline, a puffed midriff with a sloping middle ruffle and a blue sash—light blue like Porter's eyes. For my hair there was a white cloth dove. I thought, *Just like my new life—flying high and free.* Since weddings were solemn occasions, I had to wear my black high-button shoes instead of my white satin slippers.

I don't remember much about the ceremony. My eyes were fixed on Porter and my thoughts were on tonight—not having to be alone in the dark. Porter told me he didn't have a ring. "I spent all my money on the engagement party and on buying the place, Inie."

I said that was all right, but I *did* want a ring ("Not hardly married without one," I overheard Ma say to Pa). I tried not to let my disappointment show.

After the wedding was a complete supper. "Ma really outdid herself," Carl said, as he stuffed another ham sandwich in his mouth. Porter and I couldn't eat much. Porter seemed more nervous than I have ever seen him. *Probably all the excitement,* I thought.

Carl had tied some old horseshoes on the back of the buggy. They ruined our chances of getting away quietly. We were visiting Aunt Sadie for our honeymoon. We settled back for the long drive ahead. Porter squeezed my hand. We still hadn't kissed—there would be time for that later.

Aunt Sadie wanted to know all about the wedding and Porter, always anxious to talk, described everything from the preacher's wobbly Adam's apple to the icing on the wedding cake. I couldn't concentrate on any of it. My mind would slip in and out. I was making a transition from my dreams to actually sitting here next to this tall, handsome man who was my husband.

Finally Porter shoved away from the table and said, "Well, we've had a big day. Right, Inie?"

I smiled up at him, still half in my dreams.

"Yes. Well, follow me." Aunt Sadie led us down a mahogany hallway with brass candleholders lining the walls. "This is my best bedspread," Aunt Sadie said as she lit the candle in the center of the room. "Sorry I don't have extra lamps, but I figured you wouldn't be reading anyhow." Porter never even blushed, but I was glad for the darkness. When my face felt hot like it did then, I knew it was a bright shade of pink.

The door clicked behind her, and Porter locked it. I stood still, turning on my heels. Yes, this was what I had imagined—from the candlelight to the pictures on the wall. One was filled with trees like the yard in Oklahoma where we met. Another had mountains (*Which ones?* I wondered) with a small village in the foreground.

Porter came up behind me and put his arms around my waist. "Would you like to go there, Ina?"

I could hardly speak. My body felt like I had been standing too close to the stove. I folded my hands over his, "Yes, Porter, I would."

"Then you shall." He whirled me around, touching the curls on my cheek as if he were picking the bright orange poppies which grew in our yard. I had only time to think, *So this is the kiss,* before his lips were on mine. He drew back to look in my eyes as if trying to read my thoughts.

"Better than dreams," I said as he drew me close again.

Later that night as Porter lay sleeping, I watched the candle melt down smaller and smaller. I knew I should get out of bed and blow it out. After all, why should I mind the darkness now with Porter here? But I just couldn't. I pulled the blanket tighter around me. I thought Porter would take this fear from me, but he hadn't. Somehow the darkness had gotten inside.

It was too deep for him to reach.

CHAPTER 14

Fall, 1903

AS NEAR AS I CAN FIGURE, the baby was begun on our honeymoon. "Probably the first night," Porter said.

It wasn't hard for me to guess from my symptoms what was wrong with me. Ma was in the family way with her seventh, and I still remembered her throwing up with Cora. I also remembered that after about two months, you felt like living again. So I tried to get through the best I could. It was part of my daily routine. Before breakfast I'd feed the chickens and, on my way back to the house, throw up. After that I would feel fine. I don't know if Porter even knew. Ma had taught me not to complain.

I wasn't scared about taking care of a baby. I had helped Ma plenty, but Porter seemed nervous. He kept worrying about my health and who came to see me and who I went to see and if anybody had any diseases I could get. It pleased me that he was so concerned, but as I found out later there was a much deeper reason than just being a nervous father.

We weren't moved in very long when Porter got a letter from his ma. She wanted to meet me and couldn't wait any longer. Porter's father had to stay on their farm near Scottsbluff. So Porter's sister, Hulda, and her husband were bringing her to visit.

I was surprised that Porter's ma was such a fat lady because Porter was so tall and skinny, but then I found out she was his stepmother. She was as good-natured as she was wide. Hulda was big, too, but only because she was in the family way.

We found lots to talk about. Since that was *her* first baby, she was as excited as I was. Frank, her husband, was young—eighteen, like Hulda. Since Hulda was two months from her time, they figured it was safe to travel.

The morning they all had planned to leave, Hulda's pains began. Porter went for my ma. Porter's ma said, "It must be false labor," but we weren't taking any chances. Since Frank was all in a tizzy, Porter took him with him to fetch Ma.

She was sure a welcome sight. "I never had any baby come this early," Ma said, flinging off her cape, "Sure hope I can do something." Ma was gonna say more but saw Frank in the corner weeping like a child.

Ma came out a minute later. "Inie, boil some water. This baby's gonna come." Frank was still weeping. Porter had left. For the next few hours, I didn't have much time to think about why Porter deserted. Ma needed Hulda's ma and me to help. I sure got a close look at childbirth, and I wasn't sure I wanted to go through it. Ma said, "Inie, you won't be having a hard time like this."

Unless it comes early, I thought to myself. When Hulda's screams had subsided and it looked like the baby was going to be all right, Porter magically reappeared.

"Sure a little one," Frank said to Hulda, "but I'm so thankful she's all right. We're beholding to you, Clara." He paused. "Say, Clara would be a nice name for her."

I could see Ma was really tickled. Ma said the way I had helped her, maybe I ought to be a midwife, too.

"Well, let me try having my own baby first and see how I do, Ma." I was pleased with Ma's remark. She was saying something else, but I didn't hear it.

The next thing I remember was Ma bending over me holding a wet cloth on my head. "I think all that blood and pain was too much for somebody with child," Ma was saying to Frank.

Frank? I thought. *But where is Porter?*

As if Ma read my thoughts she said, "Porter's gone to the neighbors for supplies."

What supplies? I thought. *We don't need anything.* Ma made me stay in bed.

Porter came back saying, "I figured with a new baby in the house, we'd need some more things. Thought I should go while your ma's still here."

Sounds reasonable, I thought, but I turned my face to the wall and cried. Would Porter be with me at the birth of my first child, or would he run off? I wasn't anxious to find out.

Hulda and the baby and Frank and Porter's ma went home in a few weeks. I forgot my fears about Porter. He was so sweet and loving.

The fall was a busy one, but working next to Porter was like working in a dream—it never seemed hard. Porter thought the harvest went well. I was planning what we'd do with all the money. Of course, we'd put some away for our first baby. I even labeled a jar "Baby Baker" just for that purpose. After the last crop was harvested and taken to town, Porter came home—smiling like a tomcat that had swallowed a fat mouse.

Before I could ask him anything about the harvest money, he whipped out a package from behind his back. Gold paper again—a ring, and it fit just right.

"Now you're married, my dear," Porter bent down for a quick kiss. He had lots to tell me. "I was gonna wait for your birthday, but seeing as how it's only a week away, I thought I could give this to you now." I was glad about the ring and twirled it around whenever I thought about it, but I was waiting all night for Porter to bring out the rest of the money for us to count. When he didn't, I asked about it.

"Oh. Well, I put it toward a surprise."

Porter left the room so suddenly I knew he wasn't about to give me any hints on what the surprise was. In the past his surprises had been pleasant (and all for me), so I figured I didn't have anything to worry about.

I enjoyed waiting for the baby to come. Having time to be alone with Porter I knew wouldn't happen again till our kids were all grown and gone. I didn't know when I've ever been happier than sitting next to Porter doing my mending while he read the paper or drew diagrams of his inventions. I was proud of his always trying to think of a clever way to do things. I liked him to explain, but they were hard to understand. When the baby would kick, I would reach over and place Porter's hand on my stomach so he could feel the baby move.

Porter didn't talk about God like Pa and Sam did. Somehow church came too early for us with all our chores to do. I didn't know why this should bother me about Porter—especially with the way I felt about religion—but it did.

Spring came, and a lot of our leisure time melted with the snow. Porter wouldn't let me do much since my time was only a couple of months away. The fact that I couldn't even carry water put extra work on Porter. His invention sketches were put away. Sometimes he fell asleep right after supper.

Porter wanted to make sure a doctor could come, but I told him Ma had delivered over a hundred babies, which was probably more than most doctors. So Ma was going to stay with me beginning in May. Since Ma was still nursing Tom who had been born in November, he'd be coming too.

May 9 was bright and sunny. *Just the kind of day I'd like our first son to be born on,* I thought as I tied back the yellow curtains in the kitchen. Porter had

130

gone out to the fields, and I was just setting down with Ma for a cup of coffee when I felt the first of the pains.

"Ma, the baby's coming," I said.

Ma put Tommy on the floor and ran outside to call Porter, but I didn't have another pain till they were back. Porter was to stay close to the house now in case he needed to watch Tommy. Porter was certainly excited and anxious, too. Ma noticed this and sent him out to chop wood.

Ma got me settled in bed with both pillows under my head and shoved a book in my hands. It was hard to read and keep my mind on it, but Ma said the baby might take a long time to come, and I needed to be relaxed and think of something else.

About noon Ma took off her watch and laid it on the nightstand next to the bed. The pains were two minutes apart, Ma said. Porter was in the next room with Tommy. I could hear his giggles.

Porter's going to be a good father, I thought just before another pain came. Ma said to count to keep my mind off them, but I decided that wasn't enough help for me. I wished Porter could be with me, but fathers were never allowed at births. I was thankful for my Ma's being here.

I thought I'd better go into my dreams. If I could get deep enough into them, maybe the pain would fade. So I began dreaming about my family. I'd have a lot of boys for Porter and some girls for me. We'd have pounds and pounds of nutmeats every Christmas, real ponies for the boys, china dolls for the girls. I wanted an Oriental rug. "Rich ideas," Ma would have remarked had I spoken my thoughts aloud. I was just giving Porter a jeweled gold watch in my Christmas dream when the pains got worse. Now there was no retreat. *Christmas carol*, I thought and mentally began going through the words of "Silent Night." After I'd gone through all the carols, Ma said it was time to push.

"I can see the head," Ma shouted. Well, I pushed real hard because I reckoned the baby wanted to be out of this carrying on as bad as I did.

"A boy!" Ma said, as she wrapped him up and placed him next to me in the bed. Porter came in after the baby's bath. He kissed me right in front of Ma.

"He's gonna be a handsome one, just like you, Porter."

"Oh, Inie, you're the prettiest you've ever been. What shall we name him?"

"Do you like Clinton, Porter?"

"Sure, a nice name—a gentleman's name. He'll be a fine one."

Ma stayed on for a few weeks till I got on my feet. Clintie became the center of our life together. His first smile happened on Porter's lap. We were happier than ever, although at night I missed lying close to Porter since baby Clintie slept between us.

Grandma Sarah came to get her picture taken with Ma and Tommy and me and Clintie. She entertained Porter with her stories of her relative, Daniel Boone. "Some men just can't stay put but gotta try new things all the time," Grandma Sarah was saying. I looked at Porter. *Is he one of those?* I wondered. Funny thing, I

132

didn't want to stay put either before Clintie was born. He changed my mind on a lot of things.

Ma talked Grandma out of wearing her dust cap for the picture. I hoped my hair would still be brown when I was sixty-five.

I hadn't heard any more about Porter's "surprise" until the next harvest rolled around. I had forgotten it myself until he came back from town empty-handed again.

"Uh, Porter, did the money go toward that same surprise?"

"Yep." Porter left the room again. So my "Baby Baker" jar had only a few coins in it—leftover change from Porter's pocket that I emptied out before washing his breeches on the scrub board.

November 12 we went to another Hesser reunion. Halfway through we began talking about next year's reunion. It would be Grandpa and Grandma's fiftieth anniversary. "Just think, Porter, for our fiftieth anniversary I'll be sixty-five and you'll be seventy-six."

"Think we'll last that long, Inie?" I looked at Porter. He was teasing, of course, but then his eyes had that intent look that they had when he was thinking really hard over his inventions.

Uncle Ike's wife, Fannie, died a few days after the reunion. This saddened Christmas for all of us, thinking about Ike and his three boys being alone. Porter wouldn't go to the funeral with me. He wouldn't even visit the house. Was it because he had lost Tibby and their baby? For weeks after that he'd check on me all during the day and follow me around. I wished he could pray about his fears like Pa would have.

Porter got a big tree for Christmas. We strung popcorn and cranberries, and I used the gold paper I had saved from the ring box to make a star. Clintie kept us amused by trying to pick the popcorn off the tree. Three days after Christmas, just as Porter had stopped following me around so much and was returning to his old self, we got the news Uncle Bill and Aunt Lollie's baby—only three weeks old—had died. Porter wouldn't go to that funeral, either. Then he began waking up at night to check on Clintie. His "checks" would wake up Clintie next to me and then we'd all be up.

One morning when I was particularly weary, I complained to Porter, "Clintie's not going to die like Zola, Porter. Just settle down and pray about it."

Porter was mad. "Don't talk about dying to me! And as for praying—that does no good."

Porter's anger upset me, but more than that, I was concerned about what he had said. Before, I thought he was just too occupied with making a living, but now I knew it was something deeper. He was bitter, worse than me.

There wasn't any fiftieth anniversary for Grandpa and Grandma. Grandpa died the next spring. He had had ten years of preaching. "More than most," Pa said. Grandpa wanted these words on his stone: "Here lies the great faring missionary's body to wait the morn of the resurrection." Porter went with me to this funeral. I guess it was only young wives' and small

134

children's funerals that he didn't go to. Just as I was getting discouraged about all the deaths this year, I started throwing up again before breakfast. Clintie had turned a year old and was toddling around.

"Time for another one," Porter said. I wasn't so sure, having just scrubbed out a bucket of diapers on the washboard. But Clintie needed a little playmate, even if it meant more work.

CHAPTER 15

Summer, 1905

CLINTIE'S FIRST BIRTHDAY WAS A grand time. Porter and I were mighty proud when he took his first step on his birthday. He walked toward Pa, which pleased his grandpa just fine.

All summer Clintie played in the garden while I weeded. Porter said he was good company for me while he was working in the fields.

Clintie liked to trace the bugs on the leaves with his fingers. He liked the bugs—a little too much. I had to reach into his mouth to rescue one poor ladybug.

There was only one sad part of that summer. After Clintie's first birthday, there seemed to be a shadow over Porter's mind. He was especially gloomy whenever he played with Clintie. He'd be jostling him on his shoulder or rolling a ball to him when suddenly he'd hand him to me and walk out the door. He usually wouldn't come back till Clintie was in bed, asleep. I didn't understand why Porter was acting so peculiar, and when I tried to bring it up, Porter shut up tighter than a drum.

After harvest that year Porter finally told me what his surprise was: "Inie, I've bought some land."

"That's fine, Porter. Maybe you could hire Carl to help you farm it."

"It's not around here, Inie." I felt like I'd been hit in the stomach. I slowly lowered myself in the chair, not sure I had heard right.

"What'd you say, Porter?"

"This land, Inie, it's by my Ma and Pa's place."

"Porter, that's hundreds of miles away!"

"Well, Inie, I thought you liked adventure. When we were courting you were just chawing at the bit to travel and see places."

"That was before—"

"Before Clintie." Porter finished it for me.

I was crying, thinking about leaving Ma and Oklahoma. Porter looked at me and said, "Inie, you've changed." I heard the door slam behind him. I was thinking, *He's the one who's changed.* The older Clintie got, the more woeful Porter was. He didn't seem as happy about the new baby's coming, either. Whenever I said, "Porter, wanna feel the baby kick?" he'd mumble something about checking on the live-stock and leave the room.

We didn't talk about the new land in Nebraska for awhile. I thought that maybe since I'd cried, Porter had given it up, but I was wrong.

"Inie, I'll be going up to check on the land before we move there."

I wanted to throw myself at his feet and scream, "Porter, don't leave me alone. I can't stand the dark without you." But Porter knew nothing about my closet nightmares. I thought he'd laugh at me for being childish; so instead I just said, "When you leaving, Porter?" as if I were asking how the chickens were.

"Right after your birthday."

"Gonna stay for Clintie's year-and-a-half birthday?"

"No." Porter left the room again.

So as fall wore on and the days grew colder, Porter and I drew farther and farther apart. I was thinking of the glorious fall when we were courting. Was it just three years ago?

Porter thought I'd be safer at Ma's while he was gone. *Safer from what?* I thought, but I was glad he suggested it. Ma would be good company.

"Will you be back before the baby's born?"

Porter's face grew dark. He frowned. "I don't know, Inie. Look, Inie," he grabbed my hand, "I want to explain about all this. I really—I don't understand myself sometimes. I want you to promise me you won't go out alone after dark for any reason."

"I promise."

"That's my girl," Porter's old smile returned. The day Porter left I had a cold chill running up and down my spine like the ague. I was afraid it might be malaria and told Porter so.

Pa and I had had malaria two summers in a row

138

when I was a child—cold chills so intense we'd shake the bed and, then get blazing hot. Pa had said, "At times I was afraid I'd die and other times I was afraid I wouldn't."

I thought this would make Porter stay, but he seemed all the more determined to leave. "Don't you see, Inie? I just can't stay now."

I didn't say it but I thought, *You mean you can't stay because I might die and you'd have to come to my funeral.*

I didn't have malaria, but I did have my old nightmares. I had thought Porter would never leave me when I married him. I had been wrong. I wondered in what other ways I was wrong about him.

It was good being home again although I missed Porter every day. I kept my promise about not going out at night. It took them a long time to get there, but Porter's letters were full of news about the new land and full of questions about my health and Clintie's. "Seems unnatural to be so concerned," Ma would say after I read her one of his letters.

Ma and I would talk at night in the quiet when all the children were bedded down. Pa would be reading and we'd be sewing. "More talking than stitching," Pa would say with a chuckle. I loved these talks with Ma. Since Porter and I had grown apart these last few months, I didn't realize how much I missed just talking and listening to another adult voice.

Ma told me lots about herself—her courting before marriage, her faith, and her fears. One night Ma told me marking stories. I'd heard about these before but never had heard any firsthand.

"You know how Lulu got that dark bluish birth-mark on her leg? I saw a snake slither across the barn floor. I screamed and stood shaking, my hands on my legs, when Miltie got there. Course you've already heard the story about Tom's markings."

"Yes," I thought back. Lulu had been playing behind Pa's wagon when the brake gave way. Ma ran out and saw the blood dripping from Lulu's forehead, and poor little Tom had those three bright red birthmarks on his forehead.

"But here's a story you haven't heard. When we were coming to Oklahoma, I attended a nursing case," Mama began.

"I remember, Ma. What happened, anyway? You never did talk about it."

"It scared me too much, Ina. I shudder even now when I think about it. Yet I can't deny it happened because I was there." I set my sewing down and looked at Ma. She had a faraway look in her eyes. I wasn't sure I wanted to hear what she had to tell.

"I never told anyone, even your Pa," she said.

"Maybe it will be healing for you to tell it, Ma." *Maybe it would also be healing for me to tell Porter about my closet nightmare*, I thought.

"Well, when I got to the house I saw that this man, Hank, had married an Indian squaw. Dark hair and kind of haunting eyes; I can see them now." Ma paused and began again, "I could see her time was coming soon; so I told her to start pushing the baby out. The head came out nice and round, but when I felt the back it was coarse and thick, not like the usual blood plastered around a newborn. I gasped as the little fellow came out. Along his spine, about an inch thick, was a strip of fur. I wrapped him up real quick, hoping to delay her finding out, but it was the first thing she felt for. She handed him back, sobbing, 'Take him away. Take him away.' I looked for Hank, and asked for an explanation.

" 'I'm a hunter,' he said. 'I clean my pelts and leave them behind the woodpile to dry. How'd I know Star would go out there, her in a family way and all? She never should've been going after wood.' Then he asked, 'Can it be cut off?'

" 'You'll have to ask a doctor,' I told him. 'The important thing now is to talk her into feeding him, or he won't live to see a doctor.' Well Hank tried, but he came out of her room cussing. So I tried—listened to her tears, pled for the baby's life, and watched his mama doze off and on. Finally toward dawn she asked for him. I left as he was nursing. Hank was so grateful he gave me that Indian blanket plus twenty dollars.''

We both sat for a while, just rocking and thinking. I was wondering what that little fellow looked like now. As for me, I wasn't going to any barn or woodpile while I was carrying this child.

As winter settled in, nothing eventful happened. My biggest concern was Clintie's screaming too loud in church, but in light of the marking stories, that was a minor fear.

Porter sent gifts for Christmas and promised he'd be home soon, but the days went by and he didn't come. Finally, in early February, another letter came: "The blizzard has been a bad one, Inie,'' he wrote. "I've been wanting to come home. Reckon Clintie will remember his daddy?'' Tears came to my eyes. ''Porter, I miss you so much,'' I whispered.

Milton came easier. Ma said, ''The second one always does.'' I'd vowed if I had another boy I'd name him after Pa, Thomas Milton. He was sure pleased.

It wasn't more than ten days after that when Porter returned. I remember because Ma wouldn't let me get out of bed to greet him at the door. It was one of those sunny days when the icicles melting off the roof reminded you of spring. I was thinking back to another day when the world was melting, the day Porter proposed, when Pa yelled, ''Porter's here!'' I stood on the bed looking out. Yep, I could see the wave of his hair and his gray hat, but he was moving mighty slow. He even walked slowly into the house. *Something's wrong,* I thought.

''Inie's in there,'' I heard Ma say.

Porter opened the door and ran to the bed, lifting me up and twirling me around. He was kissing me all over my face and hands.

''Porter, Ma might come in.''

Porter ignored my warning and went right on. ''Oh, Inie, you're all right, and the baby's alive!'' Porter set me down to pick up Miltie.

''Of course. What did you think, Porter?'' I was puzzled.

Clintie came running in, and Porter swung him around and hugged him. ''My little man.'' He repeated over and over, ''Almost two, almost two,'' as if being two was the most astonishing thing in the whole world.

There was more than just a homecoming going on here, and I had to find out. That night I did.

"Inie, you see I couldn't bear losing a wife—not again." Then I knew he was thinking about Tibby. "And Clintie." Porter's eyes grew misty.

"Tibby's child, Porter?"

"Yes. He was a year and a half." Now I knew why Porter dreaded Clintie's reaching his eighteen-month birthday.

"And Tibby, was she in the family way?" I took a guess here.

"Yes." So Porter couldn't bear to wait around and watch his second wife and child die. His fear forced him away.

"I was looking for a new homestead. Tibby caught a chill and before I got back, they buried her. It seems she saw a man outside who scared her so much she hid behind the shed till morning," he said, *So that was why he had made me promise not to go out at night!* Things were falling into place. Porter talked some more about Tibby and his baby boy. In the end he was sobbing in my lap like baby Martin did when his pony died. I was sobbing, too. Tears of forgiveness released the bitterness I had built up toward Porter.

In spite of having two babies between us in bed that night and being even farther away physically, we were closer—closer than we'd ever been. I fell asleep thinking of something Pa always said, "If you want to heal hurts, Inie, pour in love, pour in love."

CHAPTER 16

Summer, 1906

PORTER WENT TO CHURCH THE very next Sunday. Had he forgiven God for Tibby and his child since I was all right? I don't know, but we never missed a Sunday till we moved in May.

I didn't mind moving nearly as much as I had thought I would. Maybe it was because I had my old Porter back and two lovely boys besides. May was a good month for traveling. I had never been on a train, and I was really looking forward to it. The sun had been shining just long enough to dry up the mud from the spring thaw, yet not long enough to make big cracks in the ground. Oklahoma summers hadn't really started yet.

The journey was uneventful, and I was glad. Porter's father seemed happy to see us. He was tall and thin like Porter, only with white hair instead of blond.

144

He was a rancher and "doing well," Porter said, but I wondered if he was doing so well why Porter's ma had to cook at a hotel in Scottsbluff.

Porter thought I'd enjoy staying with Georgie, another of his sisters, since our kids were about the same age. Georgie's husband, Carl Buckingham, had met us at the boxcar. That sounds funny, but there wasn't any depot there, just an old red boxcar. I was disappointed already. Porter was planning to build a house in town. I had never lived in town before, and I was picturing Morrill to be a big place like Guthrie or Stillwater. I thought it would be a fine house like Priscilla Newsbickle's. Just where we'd get the money hadn't occurred to me. Sometimes my dreams weren't too practical. We were there just a few days when Georgie suggested we go into town. "But my dresses, Georgie, they're so wrinkled! How can I go?"

Georgie laughed, "Nobody in Morrill is gonna care, Inie." So we got the kids all fresh diapered and loaded in the wagon. After some time we came to a little store with a post office in it. Georgie stopped and tied the horses' reins to the post in front of the store. "Why we stopping here, Georgie?"

Georgie pointed to the sign above the store. "United States Post Office, Morrill, Nebraska."

"But, Georgie, where are the stores, the livery stables, the hotels, and restaurants? Georgie, where are the people? There's nothing here but cornfields."

"Patience, Inie. Morrill has just begun."

"But I thought it was a big city."

Georgie laughed again. I didn't see anything funny about it. Georgie took the children in to look around. I just stayed in the buggy, holding Milt. I suppose Georgie thought I was being awful stubborn and maybe I was.

That night I turned my anger on Porter. "Why'd you ever bring me here, Porter?. There's nothin' here—not even a town. I'm away from all my relatives and friends, and I'm so alone. This has been the worst day of my life."

Porter came over, laid his hand on my shoulder, and said, "I know it's hard for you, Inie—" I threw off his hand and left the room. The only private place was outside.

But outside it was worse. The bright moonlight lit up the landscape for miles. And for miles, as far as I could see, there were no trees. *If only I could go down to Orchard Pond*, I thought. *I would find comfort there*. But there was nowhere to go, not even a bush in sight. I ran behind the barn and, leaning up against it, wept till there were no more tears in me.

After I dried my eyes, I tried to keep my sorrow to myself. The boys didn't seem to mind Nebraska. They enjoyed playing with the Buckingham children— Gayle, Mabel, and Earl. When the house that Porter built was ready, I almost hated to move out of Georgie's for their sakes.

After my disappointment over Morrill, I knew I shouldn't expect big things in a house. Sure enough, the dream of a big house was dashed, too. Porter had explained that he was expecting to get some land to homestead outside of town; so we would have to settle for something small for a while. The house wasn't any smaller than our home in Oklahoma—two rooms—but it wasn't easy living between the icehouse and the lumberyard. And there were no trees in the yard. Even though I knew we'd be leaving soon, I thought I would just go crazy without some trees. So I begged Porter, and he went down to the river to get buckberry bushes. "Crazy thing," he muttered as he hauled them from the wagon, "we probably won't be around to get any berries off of 'em."

There were seven families in Morrill then. That meant only seven women, and all the rest, not counting the children, men, coming in to file land claims. The lumberyard was doing a great business. Porter was a little concerned about living next to it, but I enjoyed watching all the commotion. It took my mind off being homesick.

One morning when I went out to the coal pile, there was a body lying out there. I thought he must be dead, but I was too scared to check; so I ran in and got Porter.

"Lucky for him he got drunk in the summer," Porter said, feeling his pulse, "or he sure would have been dead, lying out all night." I was so scared to go out to the coal pile after that I only went when Porter was home. But one time I had to have some more wood for supper. Porter would be home and hungry, so saying a prayer, I went out. It was just dusk so the lumberyard had closed down. The air was heavy and unnaturally still from midsummer heat. Then I saw him, right in front of me. He grabbed my wrist before I could go. "Look, I don't mean no harm. I'm looking for a woman to make me a bed tick." He let go of me as he saw the fear drain away from my eyes. "I didn't mean to scare you."

So it turned out all right, but Porter decided to get a dog after this second scare. Clintie loved Stripe. (He insisted on "Stripe" when he saw his spots. He always got those words mixed up). Stripe was a playful thing and quite a barker. "His size don't matter," Porter said. "His bark will scare anyone away."

Stripe barked whenever we had storms. Since we lived up on a hill where the wind really whipped around, this was a lot of barking. One night in August, the wind was really whistling. I was afraid it might be a tornado, but Porter said, "Don't usually have tornadoes around these parts." Stripe began barking so loud we could hardly hear the wind the wind or the thunder, but we did hear a loud crash. Clintie and Milt woke up crying. We didn't know if it was the lumber building or the barn. They were both in the same direction.

Porter wanted to check but I said, "Don't go—if it was strong enough out there to take a building down, no telling what it could do to a man." Porter sat down, rocking Miltie while I laid Clintie back down. We didn't do much sleeping that night. I sure didn't want anything to happen to our cow, old Bess. Besides giving us fresh milk and butter, she was a friend—the closest friend I had here. I told her everything while I was milking her. She'd swish her tail and turn her head back and moo as if she were really listening.

The next morning as soon as it was light, Porter

went out. "It was the barn, wasn't it?" I could tell from Porter's face.

"Yep."

"The cow. Is Bessie dead?"

"Couldn't find her—must've run off."

I don't think we ever would have found her if Porter hadn't taken the short cut home that day. "I found Bessie," Porter was washing his hands, his back toward me.

"Porter, that's wonderful! Fresh milk again." I was really thinkin' about those long talks with Bessie.

Porter turned around, reaching for the towel, "She's dead, Inie, but it wasn't the storm that did it. She was shot right through."

"Who'd do such a thing?" But I knew it was probably just one of those nameless drunks. Probably thought Bessie was a deer. I was awful mad but then maybe I'd drink, too, if I was all alone in this disappointing town.

Days seemed terribly gloomy as fall came. It didn't help matters to hear that Pete and Lucy Matthews got married on September second. Missing the wedding, plus all the memories of the play parties I'd gone to with Pete and Lucy, really got me down. Some nights after my closet nightmare I'd wake up sobbing, not just from my dream, but from loneliness. I was glad Porter was a sound sleeper. It didn't do any good to bother him. He had enough trouble trying to line up a homestead. Homesteading was his dream, and I'd try to be patient and fit into it.

Just when I thought I couldn't stand it any more,

Lottie and Ide Castille came. I was so excited when Porter said we'd have company that I put on my engagement frock. I hadn't dressed up in months since there wasn't any church here. I made a lemon drop cake and big sugar cookies.

Lottie had a smooth face, kinda plump, with spit curls on her cheeks. Ide was short, too, with a full beard. Since they were older than Porter and me, I wondered why they didn't have any children. The way they fussed over Clintie and Milt I knew they must have wanted some. Aunt Lottie, as we began calling her, started coming by two or three afternoons a week. She'd rock Miltie to sleep, and then stay and chat with me about everything and about everyone she knew. She became my friend, my older sister, and, at times, my mother. Since Uncle Ide had opened the first pool hall in town, I decided pool halls couldn't be as bad as everyone said. And the men here needed something to do besides getting drunk.

Christmas was a blue time. I couldn't help thinking back to Christmases when I was little. My present would be on a chair next to the fireplace. My stocking would be filled with oranges, apples, and sweet nut-meats. The immediate fact was that this year was going to be a slim one. Porter had told me, "Our money—the savings we got from selling our Oklahoma property—is running out. I can't finagle a deal on some homesteading land." When Uncle Ide and Aunt Lollie came with presents and a turkey the gloom seemed to lift.

The bread I baked, plus Aunt Lottie's weekly hams, kept us going.

"Now don't thank me." She'd bustle into the room. "Thank all those boys playing so much pool. Now where's my boys?" she'd ask. And with that Clintie and Miltie both would come running to scramble for a place on her lap.

But not even Aunt Lottie could save us forever. Porter came home one day particularly depressed. I thought maybe it was the weather. It seemed like we hadn't had a single day of sunshine in February. "Inie, I've given up," Porter said. I felt guilty for being glad. Maybe we'd move back to Oklahoma now. "Even if a homestead did come through, now we haven't got the money to build a house on it. So I've taken a job putting bridges over the tri-state ditches every mile for the Pueblo Ditch Company. You'll be cooking for the men."

I had a lot of questions about it, but my first one was, "When do we start?"

"March." March, that was next week. Not that I had gotten so attached to this house on the hill, but now that we'd be living in a tent, I sure hated to leave our home. Of course we had to give Stripe away—ditch camps moved every three weeks. The boys cried awful about it, and I did too; but I think I was crying mainly for myself.

CHAPTER 17

Spring, 1907

MARCH WAS A COLD MONTH, and I was worried the boys would catch a chill.

I never had been so busy in my life—cooking for twelve men with the boys tugging at my skirts, always begging to go down and watch the "big shovel." It was really a scraper that would dig out the dirt, a great big scoop hauled by team of horses.

Porter had brought our team of horses with him; so he made five dollars a day. My wages were two dollars a day—sixty dollars a month. In the afternoons I'd do the wash. Sometimes the water would freeze while I left it out to go cook lunch. I'd hang the wash on tent ropes or barbed-wire fence. Sometimes it would take two days to dry. I smiled to myself when I thought how Ma would say that the "Good Man must have been looking out for us or we would've got pneumonia for sure.'' Water had to be hauled. Dinners had to be carried from the kitchen tent to the dining tent. Miltie, not yet two, would toddle along, or stay in the tent when I could talk Clintie into watching ''baby brother.''

Every three weeks the camp would move. This meant even the married men didn't have their wives with them. Porter would take them to the closest town on Saturday night. I'd chide Porter for this; I'd had enough of drunk men in Morrill, but he'd say, ''Inie, the men are lonely. There's nothing for them to do.'' It was the boss's drunkenness which led to his firing before we came. His wife had done the cooking. Their leaving gave us our jobs. The new boss was a good man and fair.

Some of the men were very young. Hans, the German lad, was just sixteen. He reminded me of Sam Hall, with his fair complexion and quiet ways. George and Harry were family men, always talking about their wives and only staying long enough to get some cash. Cassie was just a drifter. He always smiled at me in a way that made me turn away and avoid him. ''Pa'' Hansen was the oldest. After his wife died and his kids grew up, he was just too lonely to keep farming. They left the lightest work for him to do.

But the man that stands out the most, etched in my memory, was the big hulk, Ol' Slewfoot. We nicknamed him that because he had a husky build and so much dark hair all over his arms that he seemed like a big old bear. I guess the boys thought he was a bear, too. They'd run and pounce on him like a couple of pups on their mother. Many a time I'd see Slewfoot

153

coming to meals with Miltie on his shoulders and Clintie hanging onto his leg, riding on his foot. It was plenty big enough for a seat. Since his real name was Marion, he didn't mind being called Slewfoot. In fact his nickname saved him quite a few scrapes. Slewfoot had a hot temper, especially when he was drunk, which was quite often. Teasing him about being "Marion" would always set him off.

There were a lot of rumors about Slewfoot floating around. Some said he'd killed a man in California. Others said his wife and child died in a fire. But his past remained a mystery. Nobody had the nerve to ask him about it, and he didn't want to talk.

Toward early summer, just when I was beginning to enjoy those mornings without a chill in the air, I started throwing up again. I hated this part of it, but it was worth it when I thought of the coming baby. There was another pleasing thought about it this time. I'd get to see Ma. Of course, I'd be traveling home to have the baby. Ma was the best midwife, and besides that, she was my ma.

I didn't want any of the men to see me sick; so I'd get up before dawn to fetch water. By the time the camp was up, I'd be just fine, frying pancakes and potatoes over the stove. I always did my potato peeling at night. As each potato skin fell to the floor, I'd think about all the plush furniture I'd get for the house with my wages. Porter was gonna use his wages for the lumber to build the house. The only unpleasant thing about peeling potatoes was sitting for so long. My tailbone had been sore ever since I had Miltie.

If being pregnant wasn't uncomfortable enough, hot

breezes blew in every day, driving the dust in front of them. "Too early for it to be this hot," Porter would say, wiping his brow. By now, Porter was feeling mighty sorry for me and said maybe we ought to quit. But the wad of cash I was collecting made me reluctant to give up. I wanted furniture I could be proud of, and now I was saving for an Oriental rug. I didn't tell Porter. He might think it was silly.

Seems like Miltie, young as he was, sensed how tired I was and tried me even more than usual. In normal times, in our own house, I could have coped with him better. I did remember that Clinton, at just over a year, was a little fiesty, too.

Milt would get mad at me for not taking him on my lap while I was cooking. He'd tug and tug on my skirt and then throw himself down and kick. None of these stunts worked, since twelve hungry men were coming in to be fed. But the clever little rascal, finally found a way to get my attention. He held his breath, and it scared me so I dropped what I was doing and picked him up.

Eventually I decided to ignore him, hoping he'd find another trick. I still wanted to keep an eye on him pretty close though. One day, about midmorning when I was washing chickens for lunch, Miltie pulled on my skirt. After a few tugs, he began holding his breath. I kept on washing chickens, glancing at Miltie occasionally. Once, when I looked, he was gone! I found him lying in front of the tent, shaking all over with spasms, still holding his breath. I carried him back into the tent and threw my chicken water on him. That cold water shocked him back into breathing,

Slewfoot said. I never had such a scare. I knew I'd just go crazy if I ever lost one of my children.

It was Slewfoot who gave us the next scare. He and the boys had been into town the night before for their usual spree. Clintie had gotten up early on Sunday, having decided he'd try fetching the water today. He came running in screaming, "Slewfoot's dead! Slewfoot's dead!" Miltie began crying, not because he knew what *dead* meant, but because he knew from Clinton's voice that something was awful wrong. As Porter and I hurried to him, I kept thinking that there wouldn't even be any relatives at his funeral.

Porter knelt down close to his face and said, "He's breathing."

So he's just drunk, I thought. *Now to explain to Clintie.*

"Slewfoot was just so tired he lay down and fell asleep right here."

"Yes, honey. You know how you feel sometimes after supper when Daddy has to carry you to bed." Clinton nodded his head, relief written all over his little face. "Pretty soon he'll wake up and we'll all have breakfast. Now come on back to the tent." Clint followed, every now and then looking back at Slewfoot.

By mid-July Porter said we were definitely quitting. He had enough money for our house. I was very happy. He swung me around and kissed me right on the mouth in front of all the men. Some of them smiled and turned away. There was a little tug on my thoughts that night as I was counting my money. *Will I*

156

have enough for an Oriental rug once the rest of the furniture is ordered?

We said our good-bys and packed up. There was a sorrowful parting between the boys and Slewfoot. For his sake I hated to leave. His dark-tanned body bore more than a few scars. Whatever life he'd had before must not have been happy. Porter said Slewfoot no doubt would lie in an early grave. Years later, rocking my babies, I'd think about big old Slewfoot and wonder if he were still alive, still getting drunk and still working for the Pueblo Ditch Company. Then I imagined him meeting some strong, heavy-set woman and being content to farm and have boys of his own clinging to him. I'd try to hold that picture in my mind instead of seeing him lying dead drunk on the ground.

CHAPTER 18

Summer, 1907

HOMESTEADERS HAD TO LIVE ON THE LAND for five years before claiming it. That meant we'd be staying put to "prove" ourselves and that was good news to me.

When we got on our land, we lived in a tent till Porter got the house raised. His Pa and Uncle Ike and some of the neighbors helped him. He put the finishing touch on the house while I was in town, "So it would be a surprise," he said. The surprise was a star etched on the wood above the door and painted white. "Does it remind you of looking up at the stars at summer play parties, Inie?" Porter slipped his arm around my waist. I was pleased at his thoughtfulness.

Although the homestead had only two rooms, Porter said by next summer he'd have two more built in the gable above the porch. September 10 was the housewarming party. Aunt Lottie had brought a ham and some cakes from town, as well as some of her canning jars, "To fill up your new cellar," she said. Uncle Ike was also a fiddler; so we had music and food. I felt I was really going to be happy here. Still there was a terrible ache inside for Ma and Pa, but I decided it would always be there and I just had to live with it.

A week later, the furniture I had ordered from Sears and Roebuck came. Porter brought it home from town in a wagon. Moving in the tables and chairs and dresser and bed was so exciting, I almost forgot all the hard work I had to do to get it. I wasn't really terribly disappointed that I didn't have enough money for the Oriental rug because I realized having an expensive rug on a homestead was mighty silly or prideful and maybe both. It wouldn't have fit in, but when I got my big eight-room house in town, then I'd get that rug. Even as we moved into the homestead, I was planning and dreaming about that big house. Porter and I were alike in that respect. We always wanted more than we had. I don't mean we were miserable or discontented; we were just ambitious. I felt guilty about my dreams for a bigger house when I got a letter from Ma the next day telling about Uncle Jim's taking bankruptcy on his store. I wondered if he wished he was still sheriff.

One of the friends Aunt Lottie would bring out to see me was Mrs. Richards. She and I had lots to talk about since, as near as we could figure, our babies were due about the same time—on Lincoln's birthday.

I made lots of clothes for the boys that winter—little white shirts and pants to go under their skirts with

ruffles. Clintie, being "almost four," always protested (holding up four fingers), "I'm no baby. No
baby, Ma, and no girl! Uh-uh."

But I said, "Now, Clintie, when you go to school
you can wear big boy pants."

Miltie, not understanding the controversy, but still
wanting to follow Clint's lead, would just shake his
head, muttering, "No, no, no."

Porter thought I should go early to Ma's since you
could never trust the weather. So soon after Christmas
he drove us all down to the depot. He wouldn't be
going with us, since he had to take care of the live-
stock and the place. And even if he could have found
someone to feed the animals, with all the men roaming
around, we couldn't risk leaving the house for very long.

Much to my delight, the baby came right on Lincoln's birthday. Ma said, "This is a sign, mark my
words; he'll be a great man, full of honesty and spir-
itual understanding."

If that wasn't enough, Pa chimed in, "He'll probably be a preacher (I knew Pa still wanted to be one);
but if he ain't that, he'll be a man of the Book."

"So we better call him by a biblical name, like
'Enoch,' the man who walked with God," Ma said.

"Enoch," I looked down at the round little face.
"Yes, that will suit him fine," I said. With all the
wonderful things said about him, I wasn't as disappointed as I thought I'd be at having another boy.

It was wonderful being with Ma and Pa, but I sure
missed Porter. I was glad to hear he'd be coming to
take us home on the train. What I didn't know was that

Porter had another reason for coming to Oklahoma. He meant to talk Ma and Pa into moving to Nebraska to homestead. Well, I sure appreciated Porter's doing that since I had missed them terribly, but I told him they had been in Oklahoma for almost twelve years and they'd never leave. But I didn't realize the power of Porter's way with words. The picture he painted of new unsettled land glowing in the sun, just waiting for the first man to plant a seed in her rich soil, appealed to the adventure in Pa.

He worked on Ma from a different angle. I overheard it as I was nursing Enoch. He sat down next to her and admired her sewing. Then he went on and on about the dinner, "Sure am glad you taught Inie to cook as fine as you do. Makes eating a real pleasure. Yep, a real pleasure." Porter sat back, his hands hanging on his vest as if he were figuring out just how to approach it. Suddenly he leaned forward all intense, waving his hands, "Ain't Inie a picture, Ma? Those are your first grand-younguns. Too bad you're missing all their growing up."

He leaned closer and said almost in a whisper, after checking around the room for Carl or Elsie, "Wasn't Inie aways your favorite?" Ma nodded. I looked down at Enoch, as if I wasn't listening. "You know moving ain't bad—a new house, probably a bigger one to decorate and seeing your grand-younguns every day." Ma put down her sewing and looked away. Porter knew he had planted the idea and too much said would have made Ma feel like she was being pushed. Porter got up slowly and kissed Enoch on his bald little head and then said, loud enough for Ma to hear, "You sure look pretty tonight, Inie."

When Porter had left, I chuckled to myself. He sure was a politician, but I was happy about his scheming since it was for my benefit. A fast thought crossed my mind, *What if sometime his schemes aren't for my benefit?* but I shooed it away as quick as it had come.

When Enoch was three weeks old, we set out for Nebraska. We couldn't wait much longer since Uncle Ike had to come all the way from town to feed the livestock. Porter was so pleased with himself for getting Pa and Ma to agree to move that he decided to celebrate by buying me an expensive gift. He presented me with a little glass ship full of candies.

We all enjoyed the train ride. Porter held the boys on his lap pointing out "moo-cows" and, now and then, a buffalo. We even saw an Indian trying to race the train. Clintie thought that was mighty exciting.

Then at Pawnee the train came to a sudden stop—so sudden in fact that Enoch just about flew out of my lap. He was nursing under a blanket which saved him, because I was holding on to him so tight. Porter went up to find out what it was about. Some old man had been crossing the track, and being hard of hearing, he hadn't even looked for a train. He managed to jump free, but the wagon he left on the track derailed the engine and toppled the first passenger car.

Porter came to get me. "Inie, you better go see," he said. "You know about taking care of hurt folks." Taking the baby, he pushed me forward.

I didn't have time to explain that all those medicines

I recited when we were courting weren't learned through use but were copied from Grandpa Martin's storeroom to impress Porter.

As I was pushing my way to the front of the train, I was reviewing what I'd seen—Lilly, then Hettie's child's birth. True, I had fainted after Ma delivered the bloody afterbirth, but I'd be all right this time. I was older now. They were just pulling the last of the passengers out of the car when I got there. Most were just bruised, but there was a child with a bleeding forehead and a woman with a broken arm.

"Are you a nurse, Miss?" the conductor was asking. Before I could answer, he shoved some bandages in my hand and pointed to the child.

She had long blond braids, and looked just the way I pictured my own little girls one day. I had seen Ma repair Lulu's head when she had hit the wagon; so I closed my eyes to remember. Then I looked in the bandage bag for iodine. *There! Good.* The conductor was sloshing toward me with hot water. First I washed the wound, then applied iodine. The gash was deep; after the bleeding stopped, I saw how deep. It was just as well she was out—wouldn't hurt so much. There, the bandage was on. I wondered what her name was and if she were traveling alone.

The conductor came back and peered over my shoulder. "Good job." he nodded, "looks too young to be traveling alone, doesn't she?" I was wondering if I'd have to put a splint on the woman's arm but was relieved when I saw it was already done.

Porter was real proud of me when I told him and said, "You ought to take more nursing cases."

"Maybe someday I will, when the boys are grown," I said, reaching over to tousle Miltie's curls.

The train hooked up a new engine, and we were off. But I kept thinking about the girl I had bandaged, who she was and where she was going, long after we pulled into Morrill.

Enoch had Aunt Lottie for a first visitor in Morrill. She carried on and on over him, fussing and clicking her tongue, saying, "What a pretty thing you are!" Aunt Lottie sure appreciated babies. I reckon Clintie got jealous, because when she left, he bent over Enoch's crib and said, "He hain't no pretty thing." Porter and I would laugh every time we thought of it.

Soon as I felt like having my insides jostled around on a wagon again, I went to see Mrs. Richards. Her boy had been born on Lincoln's birthday, too. "He's gonna be a preacher," she said.

"I don't know how you're alive—fifteen pounds!" I looked at her small waist and hips.

" 'Twas a miracle of God. I take no credit for it. That's why I know he's going to be a preacher— God's got him marked."

What Mrs. Richards said about being marked by God got me to thinking. I didn't resent her religion; I admired it. I could learn from her, and having boys with the same birthday would give us a special bond.

Aunt Della and Uncle John came for a visit and decided to stay, with their four kids in a one-room cement house. Uncle John got a job hauling the big scraper that dug ditches. Uncle John had been poor all his life. "He just has had a hard time making a living," Porter remarked.

"I'm glad you don't, Porter," I said, rubbing my hand across the back of his neck. He grabbed me and swung me on his lap.

"When you been kissed last, Inie?"

"Not since full moon." It was what I always said.

"Well, it's high time then," he said.

With Porter's arms around me and the wavy lock of his hair falling down so softly, I'd feel that magic all over again.

At first I was glad when Aunt Della and Uncle John came, but then I decided they lived too close. It seemed she was always over here, spouting her religion. They were called "Russelites" or Jehovah's Witnesses. Once Porter made the mistake of asking what they were witnesses to. "Well, we're going to see the end of the world, of course," and Aunt Della was off, warning us with words of gloom and destruction. When she got to the fire part, Clintie would run and hide behind my skirts. The third time this happened, I ordered her out.

"Why, she moved up here just to convert me," I said. I was mad. But in a few days Aunt Della was back, as fervent as ever.

I was relieved when they began breaking ground for her kitchen—that would keep her home for a while. The next time I saw her, she was screaming, and wringing her hands. "Inie, Inie, John's gone! Is it chicken or beef? Oh, dear, we don't have either!"

"What's wrong, Aunt Della?" I had to pry it out of her, question by question.

"Snakebite!"

Thank heaven she was sane enough to tell me that much. I grabbed the chicken I had soaking in the pail (Ma would have said the Good Man arranged it again) and a rag and ran as fast as I could, leaving Aunt Della sputtering.

Hettie was lying by the new boards for the kitchen. I expect the snake had come out when they dug up the ground. Pa had killed a slew of copperheads when he was building our house in Oklahoma. I wrapped up the chicken, applied it to her leg, and sat down to wait. The sun was beating down, and I began praying—the Twenty-third Psalm (that counted as a prayer, didn't it?). It was up to me now if she lived or died—or was it? Did God take a hand in things like this? As if in answer, green pus began pouring out. I relaxed my pressing. When Uncle John returned, I went back home. Aunt Della, with Enoch in her arms, met me. "She's dead, isn't she? I just can't face it."

"No, Aunt Della, she'll be just fine." I dumped the chicken and the poultice in our garbage ditch. Porter would bury it when he got home. Well, God had come through this time—or was it just the chicken?

Summer passed and then harvest. "Pretty good for our first one, huh?" Porter held out the cash to me. That was all I was going to see of our profits. Porter was working on an invention, and all the money went for parts. This time I didn't even ask what it was. I was so tired.

"Worn out," Aunt Lottie said. "And no wonder. Three children under five and all active boys." She was right. Even Enoch, just eight months old, was crawling and pulling himself to standing.

When my twenty-second birthday came around, I felt more like sixty. I had even begun to examine my eyes for rings. I know I was crabby with the children and ornery with Porter. After we had some pretty hot words over whether or not Milt needed new shoes, he flew out one night, slamming the door behind him. Presently he was back. I ran to him, and sobbed in his arms. "Inie," he was kissing my hair, my forehead, then the tears on my cheeks, "you're not yourself. You need more sleep. Now get to bed. I'll watch the boys."

After that I went to sleep soon after supper. Porter fed the boys and got them ready for bed. I didn't even wake up when he slipped Miltie and Enie in beside me. Clintie, now four, had his own little feather tick in the corner by the stove. My body soon grew strong again.

One day in December Porter came rushing in, waving a letter. "It's your ma and pa! They're coming; they're coming!"

I grabbed the letter. Carl and Mollie were getting married on January 6, and Elsie and Paul on January 15. Then Ma and Pa would be packing up and leaving. Porter was to find a homestead for them "as close to yours as he can," Ma had written. I was sorry about not seeing Elsie—they were staying in Oklahoma— but glad Carl and Mollie were coming. The trip took them longer than I thought. It was an anxious spring for me, not receiving a letter while they were on their

167

way. I was thinking how romantic the trip would be for the newlyweds, Carl and Mollie; of course they'd be with everyone else. Lulu would enjoy having Mollie along. They were the same age—sixteen. Little Cora was ten, just the age I was when we made the trip from Nebraska to Oklahoma. Tom, at five, was just the right age for adventure. How Clintie would enjoy having him for a playmate!

It was April 4 when they arrived, over seven hundred miles, Pa said. Ma was excited to see the grandyounguns. They hadn't seen Enie since he was three weeks old, and now he was walking.

Porter and Carl helped Pa with the planting until Carl got a place of his own. Carl and Mollie were so in love, it reminded me of myself and Porter so long ago. Sometimes it seemed such a long time since we had been newlyweds. Other times, when he'd pull me close with that boyish grin and I'd look deep into his blue eyes and think, *The color of the Nehama River* while he kissed me, it seemed like only yesterday. Carl and Mollie held hands openly and even kissed in front of the children. Ma said, "This younger generation," while I couldn't decide what I thought. Porter and I kept to the old ways with private affection, but maybe more openness was healthy, and good for the kids to see sometimes. Carl and Mollie were a picture-book couple. She was a beauty and, even though he was my brother, I had to admit Carl was handsome.

That summer Ma helped me rig up a cheese press. We bent a pole spanning two trees and tied a heavy weight to it; then a gallon of cheese curds was pressed under the pole. It took three weeks but that cheese was worth waiting for. We also dried hominy and corn on sheets on our roof.

Ma and Pa hadn't been settled in the homestead long before there was a flu epidemic. They both came down with it, followed by Tom and Cora. Carl and Mollie had moved out and escaped. Doc Fox came over to tell me about it. "Inie," he said, "Lulu and Martin are killing themselves trying to take care of everyone, but the worst thing is your ma. She won't stay put. When she hears little Tommy sobbing, she goes to him. There's a saying about this flu as true as my face, 'Everybody that steps their foot on the floor dies.' Yep, that seems to be the difference between those that make it and those that don't. The ones that stay in bed live. But, Inie, you stay out of there—you got your own younguns to think about." He cocked his head to where Clintie and Milt were playing marbles in the yard.

I wondered if he was thinking of his own boys that died. Mrs. Fox had almost lost her mind, I'd heard. And Doc Fox—why, everyone said it was cigarettes and whiskey that kept him going. Aunt Lottie thought he had turned to smoking and drinking out of guilt. "I suppose he feels that he, being a doctor, should've been able to save them," she said. *Just like Dr. Martin*, I thought, *not able to save Lilly.* And then maybe he was out with so many others during that epidemic that his own boys suffered. If anything happened to Pa and Ma, I'd feel responsible since they had moved here to be near me.

Porter saw I was torn up and undecided, so he said,

"Inie, go. I'll get Aunt Lottie, and we'll manage the kids."

Calling, "Pray for me, Porter," I left. It was the most tiring few days of my life. The hardest job was managing Ma, but after a whole day of ordering her back to bed, she began to trust me to take care of Tom. I prayed hard that I wouldn't get the flu. My prayers had worked in saving Hettie; so I decided to try it again. My prayers were answered, and it was more of a miracle than I thought as I found out later when Reverend Haycroft, the new minister, came to see us.

"Inie, do you know every man who came to do the chores for your Pa got the flu? Why, a step on the property meant near-death. Two of the men, along with seven children, had died. And here you were taking care of them in the house," the preacher said.

"The good Lord sure took care of me." I surprised myself by talking about God aloud. I had never done that before.

"Well, that's exactly who I came to talk to you about. We're starting a new Christian Church, and we'd like you and Porter to attend."

"Why, sure we will," Porter said. He was resting his hand on my shoulder. "I used to be a Sunday school superintendent." That was another surprise for me. He'd never told me.

At the end of September Aunt Della and Uncle John were going back to Oklahoma. Ma was sorry to see her baby sister leave, but she understood that they felt more at home with John's folks who were also Witnesses. "If you're gonna plow on Sunday," Pa said, "you gotta be with others who do." I was sorry to see

170

her go, too, but really I had enough on my mind without thinking about the end of the world. They thanked me again for saving Hettie. The bite had been so serious that she was just beginning to walk after two months.

"Oh, don't thank me. Thank the Lord." There I was again, saying God's name. I was turning into a regular fanatic.

The highlight of 1910 was the telephone. I had seen them before at the railroad depot, but now everyone was getting them. They even hired some girls to connect up the wires. We'd ring up and say, "Central, get me—" and then give the number we wanted. We were as delighted as the boys to hear another voice coming through the wire.

Pa and Porter played checkers over the phone those long winter nights when the snow kept everyone at home. We got to know the central girls' names—Maude, Amanda, and Becca.

One day when I was in Morrill I decided it would be fun to take the boys in to see the central switchboard. I had to hold on to Enie and Milt real tight. They wanted to pull out all the wires, especially Miltie, who loved to take things apart. The central girl turned around to say hello. "I'm Maude," she said. I stared. This was the same girl I had bandaged on the train wreck at Pawnee two years before. I was sure of it. She had no idea who I was, of course. Enie sat on her lap at her invitation. Then I explained who I was.

"Say, they told me about you. You did a swell job—hardly notice the scar." She lifted up a curl of blond hair from her forehead. "I was coming to Morrill to visit my relatives, and I met my husband, Joseph Raines." She said his name real slow. "Sounds wonderful, doesn't it?" She held out her hand to show the silver wedding band. "We couldn't afford gold, but, oh, we'll be rich. Joe went to California to make a fortune. Then he'll send for me." I was fascinated by how her looks had changed in the two years—from a young girl with braids to a woman with a wedding band.

"What's on her fingers, Ma—strawberry preserves?" Clintie asked.

"Hush," I poked him.

Maude laughed. "No, it's polish, fingernail polish. Don't worry; You're a boy. You won't have to wear any," she said.

When I found out Maude had left her mother in Oklahoma, I felt sorry for her. I knew what it was like to be alone without your kin. So I invited her to the house. She became a regular guest. She was happy for me when I told her I was going to have another child.

She'd tell me her worries about Joe when she hadn't gotten a letter for a while. One time she didn't hear for about six months. She was weeping and carrying on so I made her stay the night. A few days after that, Maude was in high spirits again. Joe's ma had received a letter from a friend in California who had run into him. Joe's ma had told my ma before she'd had a chance to tell Maude; so I got to bear the news. Maude said, "Oh, Baker, you saved my life." But then as the weeks wore on, Maude became depressed again. "He must have someone else. I just know it." She was

172

crying her eyes out, rolling and unrolling her blue silk handkerchief into a ball. I wanted to tell her to pray about it. But since I was so new at praying myself, I couldn't find the words.

The next Sunday Maude didn't show up for Sunday dinner. That wasn't like her. The kids kept asking for her; so I called up the switchboard to see if she had to work.

Amanda answered.

"Maude there?" I asked.

"Is this Inie?" In a small town you got to know everyone's voice. "I'm sorry to tell you this. Maude was found dead today. She was all dressed up."

. "She was coming to our place," I said.

"Uh-huh. Well, she was lying by the buggy. Don't know what killed her."

"Thanks, Mandy," I said, stunned. I hung up.

Doc Fox said maybe it was her heart, but nobody could tell for sure.

It wasn't more than week till the mail carrier knocked on the door. Holding out a letter he said, "This here came for Maude Raines. Didn't know what to do with it and didn't feel right throwing it away. Seeing as how you were a friend of hers, I thought you'd take it."

I held it up, trying to decide if I should open it or not. It was from Joe all right, postmarked California. I looked at the date—four months ago! Why, it had been lost in the mail. It didn't seem right to open someone else's mail even if she was dead, and besides Joe had been wired to come to the funeral last week. I was sure he didn't want the letter. Why should he know that she never received it? It was all too late now—too late. I threw it into the fire.

Ma got two letters in April. The first said Aunt Flora, Uncle Jim's wife, had died in March. The second said Aunt Gertude, Uncle Wes's wife, died on April 19. Aunt Flora left eleven kids; Aunt Gertrude, thirteen. *So there, we're done for a while,* I thought. Bad things always happened in threes.

I had gotten over my throwing up with my fourth pregnancy a month ago, but now I felt sick all over again thinking about all the deaths. Maude had just turned seventeen. Aunt Flora was forty-five; Aunt Gertrude was forty-four. When would I die? I'd lie awake nights, listening to the rush of the water in the irrigation ditch by our house and hearing my Barred Rock hens crowing at midnight. I'd think about bandaging Maude, seeing those long blond braids, or Aunt Flora, a real beauty, on the arm of Uncle Jim, his sheriff's badge all shined up, or Aunt Gertrude, lying still in her grave, leaving a two-week-old baby behind. Well, I kept thinking these thoughts right on through summer. When the baby would kick, I'd place my hand on my tummy and pray, "*O Lord, give me a happy child. I just can't stand any more gloom.*"

Ma said my prayers were sure answered because she swore Lee was born with a grin on his face. *Now two more good things have to happen*, I thought, *to cancel out the bad*. I knew just what they'd be, too. I knew Aunt Lulu in Oklahoma was pregnant, and it wasn't long till Ma came over to tell me she'd had a letter and Aunt Lulu had a boy she named Enoch.

174

Then a few weeks after that Carl's wife, Mollie, had their first one and named her Clara after Ma. So now maybe the spell was broken—three new lives for three deaths. I fell asleep, listening to the water, pretending I was at the ocean front in Australia or Hawaii. I never did hear the rooster crow.

CHAPTER 19

Winter, 1911

THE WINTER OF 1911 PORTER BEGAN working on his invention sketches in earnest. One of his inventions finally got us off the homestead—an irrigation timer.

Porter would take out his pocket watch and figure how long it took to water each side of a field; then he'd set alarm clocks to that amount of time. Somehow the water would be released when the alarm went off. When the next alarm went off, the next field would get the water. This, of course, saved lots of time—not having to go out in the middle of the night and set the water in a different place. It also saved water, Porter argued, because from the size of the field, he could estimate how much water was necessary and not waste any. It sounded smart to me and I was proud of him.

Porter ran into a German fellow, named Godfrey, who was passing through Morrill. He had heard about Porter's invention and had taken a real interest in it. He said it needed perfecting before it could be sold to the public, and the only place to work on it would be Denver, the closest big city. Well, Porter was worried about my being alone out on the homestead, so he decided to move us into town. Besides, the five years we needed for proving our land was up, and all one hundred and sixty acres were ours. We'd rent out the farm and use some of that money to rent a house in town. Well, I couldn't decide whether this invention was a blessing or a curse. Right now it seemed like a curse—moving away from Ma and Pa and having Porter spend a lot of time in Denver.

We started calling our new home "the little brown house." Living in town wasn't as bad as I had feared. We weren't at all close to the lumberyard or the icehouse or the hotel and bar. We were, in fact, out in the country, right next to the city limits; and Porter was talking about getting a car so it wouldn't take any time at all to see Ma. He had drawn a picture for the boys of one that he had seen in a magazine at the barber shop. They had all kinds of questions, but long after Clint, Enie, and Lee had wandered back to their toys, Milt was there, wanting to know how it worked.

"Well, I tell you what, Milt," Porter said. "Let's take us a visit to Stillwater to see Uncle Jim. I heard they have a car there that you can ride in."

I was looking forward to this holiday as much as the boys were. Being cooped up all winter with a new baby and three active boys found me marking off the days till spring.

I always thought afterward that it was the excitement of the trip and preparations that brought on my dream the night before. I called it a dream because Porter did, but I was never sure it didn't really happen.

I tried to tell him exactly how it was. "In my dream there was a house with a gabled roof that came to an upside-down V. It had big cement steps leading up to a front porch. There was a wooden swing on a porch surrounded by bushes. The house had five bedrooms, one for us, and one for each of the boys. It was moving day for us, but I wasn't much help. There I was standing watching everyone rush around me. In my arms, I held a baby all wrapped up. I pulled down the blanket. It was a girl! *It must be mine*, I thought. *It looks so much like Porter*. The leaves were starting to fall. I walked in the front door just in time to see some men unrolling an Oriental rug—the biggest one I'd ever seen. The kitchen was as big as our whole homestead house. Some of my big sugar cookies were in a glass cookie jar. *Now, how did they get here?* I wondered. *I surely wouldn't have time to make them, with moving and all*." I paused to check Porter's reaction. "I had just reached into the jar to bite into one when I woke up."

Porter said, "I don't know, Inie, here you are—got us rich and everything. Five bedrooms!" Porter slapped his knee and chuckled, "Who ever heard of such a thing? But you finally got your Oriental rug and your girl, didn't you? Now if you could really see into the future, Inie, that would be a better invention than

178

mine and make a heap more money. Yep, a time machine—'' and Porter'd be staring off into space.

If Porter didn't believe my dream, I did. It was that real. After all, hadn't I been right about the man in the Sears catalog? Of course, I didn't tell Porter that.

It was good seeing Uncle Jim for the first time in six years. I had told Porter some of the outlaw stories Uncle Jim had told us and Porter was anxious to meet him. The boys enjoyed playing with their cousins, but they kept asking for a car ride. So we drove into Stillwater to the "Car-Ride-$1.00" stand and got in. The car had no top, and I thought I'd lose my hair for sure until the driver dug out a hat with a scarf attached for me to wear. The dirt was flying and so were we. Surely a speed of twenty miles an hour was dangerous.

But every time we stopped, Porter would hand him another dollar, and Milt would get out to help crank. When Porter got to drive it, he was sold on the car. I knew I'd never hear the end of it till he owned one himself.

Life was pleasant in the little brown house except for Porter's absences to Denver and our problems with Miltie.

I think my trouble with Milton all started after one winter when I entertained the boys with war stories about my pa's pa, Grandpa Wilson, in the Civil War. Those stories were just the spark that Miltie needed to set his imagination on fire.

After the story of Grandpa's first battle, when he hid in his tent out of fear, Milt turned up missing. We called and called and couldn't find him anywhere.

Bundling Clintie up, I told him to check outside for his brother. Clinton was thorough because he came back with one sorry-looking Milton. He had crawled inside an old ripped mattress cover leaning against the house. Since he was out of the wind and warm in all his winter clothes, he had fallen asleep. I was so glad to see him I couldn't be angry, but Porter said, "Now, he'll just hide again without telling you if you let him get away with it." Porter never lost his temper, but he gave Milt two hours every day for a week on the "chair"—sitting still with no talking. The not talking part wasn't so hard for Milt, but the sitting still was.

In the summer Milt would make "ammunition runs" for the "cause" by bouncing up and down on the spring seat in the wagon, holding the reins and pretending he was racing like thunder. *Harmless,* I thought, till he lay down on the seat ("to escape the gunfire"), and a steel bolt went right through his cheek. Pa was outside with the chores and took him straight to the doctor. Milt was proud of his bandage and called it his "war wound."

But the most dangerous game of all was when Milt fortified himself in the trenches—actually a dirt cave. One particular day, when all four boys were playing near the trench, the dirt caved in on Milton. Hearing his brothers scream, he jumped—just in time to save himself from being buried under six feet of heavy dirt. But the two feet that covered him was the deepest two feet I ever saw. Porter and the boys worked with shovels until you could see the shape of an arm and a head. Milt said afterward how sore his head was from all the shovels. "If I hadn't had a hat on," he moaned, "you would've broke my skull!"

I thought all those hours in the "chair" had made Miltie forget all this Civil War foolishness, but I was wrong. This time it wasn't his own doing though. It was the croup.

Dr. Fox said, "Get him by the stove and give him this." I looked at the label: "Syrup of Squills," just what I'd written down at Grandpa Martin's so long ago. Croup is like pneumonia. The chest fills up fast with phlegm and chokes the victim. Lots of people died with it. I was scared out of my wits. At night I'd have dreams of him, buried alive under all that dirt, trapped in the cave. Then I'd wake up to tend to him and he'd be choking on phlegm. I'd make a poultice for him and soak the rag in turpentine, lard, and kerosene. To make matters worse, Miltie even had to act out his Civil War fantasies with his illness. Claiming he had "gangrene," he'd write out messages to give to his "wife." The boys would serve as messengers. One message I intercepted had been copied from Grandpa's letters,

Miltie had scribbled, "My prayer to God is that we may live once more together on earth and live ever in the upper world—I want you to live as a Christian. I intend to live the best I can under my circumstances." The word *circumstances* gave away the source of his message. Other messages I'd read said, "I love you truly" and "I miss your red apple lips."

Well, Milt got worse—too bad to write his messages. But with a lot of prayer, he pulled through. I think the croup gave him quite a scare, because we didn't hear anything more about the Civil War.

In between visits to Denver, Porter helped build the Hotel Morrill. It was a swanky place. Porter took me there for a birthday dinner. When I saw the glass chandeliers, I asked, "Can we afford it here?"

"Don't worry, Inie, if this invention deal goes through, we'll be able to buy this hotel."

Sometimes, when I'd lie awake nights trembling because I was all alone and had just waked up from my closet nightmare, I'd think I'd be happier poor if Porter were lying next to me. Maybe the price of being rich wasn't really worth it.

Porter was more determined than ever, however. Sometimes it seemed like those times away brought us closer than ever, and other times it seemed like even when we were home we were still as far apart as Denver and Morrill. Watching Carl and Mollie, who still acted like newlyweds, depressed me. He hadn't been away from her one night since they were married. I knew I should be happy for them, but I wasn't. When I mentioned it to Porter, he said, "Inie, Carl will never have the money we're gonna have. Remember that Oriental rug." He placed both hands on my shoulders before picking up his suitcase for another trip to Denver.

Just when I thought I'd go crazy from being left again he announced there would be no more trips to Denver. *Is that good news or bad?* I thought. *Doesn't Godfrey want the invention?* Then Porter broke into a grin and picked me up as high as he could. (I swung easy, being only ninety pounds.) When I landed he stuck a check in my hands.

"Ten thousand dollars, Porter! That's more than I ever dreamed you'd get."

"But, my dear, it's not more than I dreamed of getting."

So we were rich. It was true. That night, lying next to Porter, planning my new house with five bedrooms, I forgot all about being alone.

CHAPTER 20

Spring, 1916

PORTER USED $1500 OF THE MONEY to buy the little brown house. He said it would bring in some good income from rent when we moved out.

Chris Martin was going to build the big new house with Uncle Ide doing the fine finishing, since he was a carpenter. Porter said to use the best lumber they could buy because he was "building the finest house in town for Inie." Martin sent away to Sears and Roebuck for blueprints.

I had planned to be a big part of the designing of the house, but in the spring I started throwing up again. This development, plus taking care of the boys, was plenty for me to handle. So I'd just trust Porter's judgment and stay clear. The house was close enough to ours that I could hear the pounding, day after day. It was heaven to my ears. It reminded me that this house really wasn't a dream but the real thing.

I began to believe, too, that I was going to have a girl, just like I had always dreamed. The doctor said she'd probably be born close to Christmas. I was hoping we'd be in the new house by then, but Porter said it depended on the winter weather and how early the cold and snow came.

We got word in the later summer that a tornado had destroyed the old Hesser Church. I felt terrible about that. I remembered that after a fiery sermon, Uncle Ike had led some converts over to Uncle Wes's pond to baptize them. I can't say I had too many religious memories from that church, but I remembered happy daydreams from the times I listened to Grandpa Hesser preach.

As my time grew near, Porter got Ma on a couple of false alarms. On Christmas Eve, the night she came it was snowing heavy. We weren't in the new house because the snow had started before Thanksgiving that year, but that was all right. I knew I was going to get my girl. Ma tried to calm me down during labor, "Now, Inie," she said, "it may be a boy, but there will be another time."

"Ma," I whispered between pains, "It's a girl, and there *won't* be another time."

It seemed like forever, but Ma said it was the fastest of any of the births.

When she came out, all wet and with hair matted down, Ma just couldn't believe it after four boys, but I could. I looked down into her face. I had seen it before in my dream.

A few days later we got word that nine-year-old Jessie Noe, one of our neighbor's children on the homestead, had died. She had had appendicitis and gangrene had set in. They took her to a hospital in Alliance but couldn't fight it. It saddened my days, and the thought came to me again, *A life for a life*. I knew I wouldn't want my baby girl taken—ever.

We named her Ina after me, of course, and then we added the "Rose" when Porter said that her cheeks looked just that color. We didn't call her Ina for long. One afternoon little Lee came up and leaning over her cradle said, "How's Tudy, Mom?" I don't know where he got the name, but after that we all called her Tudy.

Well, now, I was busy, so busy that Porter took over picking out the furnishings for the house. Sometimes he'd bring me a catalog when I had a moment, and I'd check some items. I remember ordering the chifforobe that way. It was a huge cabinet built for hats and coats with a long looking glass. Lucky for me I had trained Miltie in some household chores (mainly to keep him out of trouble). He could wash dishes, clean up the kitchen, and make the bed as well as any girl. Such work used up some of his energy. The boys all wanted to help with Tudy, but their "help" made dressing her take twice as long. When Tudy smiled her first smile, the boys figured she must be capable of laughing. So they'd perform all kinds of antics to get her to laugh—standing on their heads and making all manner of faces. When they weren't entertaining Tudy, they'd go over and watch the house go up.

No one was really surprised when the United States entered World War I on April 6. I was hoping no one I knew would have to go. Porter was not affected because he was already forty and had five children. They naturally took young single men first. I was afraid for Martin, being twenty-one, just the right age. Tommy, at fourteen, was too young, of course. People talked about the war a lot, but it was too far away to me to really think about seriously. Besides there were too many good things happening in my life: our house and our new baby girl.

Porter thought we needed a little holiday; so we traveled to Salem to see his pa and ma. This was a special trip because we were making it in our new car. Porter had paid five hundred dollars for the Ford. It even had side curtains to keep out the dust. It was exciting, but going twenty-five miles an hour was a little frightening.

I had never seen the house Porter grew up in. It was a square brick, a very big house with a large bay window. There was a room in back where Porter's pa kept his milk cool by running water over it. He had a knack for making money. Porter had the same knack, I reckon. Porter's pa had a farm west of Salem as well as a house in Scottsbluff and a ranch by Morrill.

We also went out to see the Yale schoolhouse that Porter attended, the same school where the Hessers had gone to school. The boys loved to hear stories about Porter's childhood—it seems that he was full of the dickens just like Milt.

We had an early heat wave in Morrill that year.

Everyone was complaining about it except me. It seems like as the days grew hotter, I just got happier. Having the house and Tudy would just make me weep for joy sometimes. I'd sit down with my coffee and think about it and pretty soon I'd be drying my eyes with the end of my white apron.

We had been going to the Methodist church since we moved into Morrill. Reverend Bryant was a good preacher, and I actually began listening to the sermons. After all, God had been awfully good to me, given me everything I'd always wanted. It was the least I could do to show my gratitude.

And then a peculiar thing happened. I can't explain it except that it must have been the hand of the Lord on me. I began to feel selfish, so selfish that I felt dirty all over. I spent more time washing my hands and taking baths, but, of course, that didn't do any good. I couldn't understand why I was so miserable when I had everything I'd always wanted. I didn't confide in Mrs. Richards or Aunt Lottie or even Ma. I thought they wouldn't understand. How could they when I didn't understand myself? I felt that there was a voice inside me saying that everything I had ever done was for myself.

Returning affection to Porter, I thought, *You're just doing this so he'll keep buying the fine furniture for your house you've always wanted.* I felt even the things I did for the children were only to make them dependent on me. Was I seeing myself and my motives in their true light? Was I really this self-centered? I decided I was and I grew unhappier with each day.

I didn't think I could be any more miserable, but

one late-June day proved me wrong. We had all gone swimming. Lee stayed close to shore, playing and splashing in the water. Pretty soon Milt came in and said they were going farther out. Enie, being nine, decided he was big enough to go with them. I wouldn't let Lee go. He pouted for a while but then started building a sand castle. Pretty soon Clint and Milt came running and screaming, "Enie's gone! We cant find him anywhere." I was terrified. There had been drownings here before. I never prayed so hard in my life. Before, when I asked God to help, I felt I was doing Him a favor to use His services. Now I felt like I was too sinful, too dirty to ask for anything, but I did anyway. I shaded my eyes with my hand. Clintie and Milt were running toward a rowboat that had beached. A crowd was gathering. Picking up Tudy, I ran toward the boat. Two men were gently carrying Enie onto the sand.

"You his ma? I pulled him out by the hair. The way this current is, I couldn't grab any other part."

Terror must have been on my face for the other man said, "Oh, he's breathing all right, but don't thank us—thank the Lord. The way he was lying in the water when we came upon him, I thought we were recovering a dead body."

I knelt beside Enie. His hair was matted; his skin a little blue, but his chest was rising in regular breaths.

After that day I still felt selfish, but God seemed closer. So I was miserable yet nearer something big in my mind—whether an idea or God, I couldn't really say.

When our church held a revival meeting with a

Reverend Williams doing the preaching, I planned to go. Of course, I wanted Porter to come with me, but he had so many business deals cooking that half the time I didn't know till an hour before if he'd be home that night. He'd gone off to Lincoln looking into something so I went to church with my two closest friends, Aunt Lottie and Mrs. Richards. Clint said he and Milt would look after Enie and Lee. So there I was, in church sitting with Tudy on my lap. I was expecting to be relieved of my misery somehow, and I tried to listen carefully. Reverend Williams was talking about how awful you feel when the hand of God is on you to convict you of sin. *Why, that's me!* I thought.

"God opens a door in your soul and you see yourself in a mirror—only you're looking at your insides instead of your outsides. The mirror is so dirty and smudged you can hardly see yourself. You don't really want to, yet there's no way you can't look. There's only one Person who can make that reflection clean and pure, true to yourself so you can look at that mirror in your soul and smile at yourself and you know who He is." The preacher went on to explain the way of salvation and believing—I'd heard it many times, but this time was like the first. I closed my eyes. I wanted to be pure inside. I wanted to make God my desire, not money or a house, or even my baby girl sleeping so peacefully in my lap. I wanted to be happy, not because of what I had, but because of who I was. A tear formed and fell down on Tudy's hair.

The pianist began playing "The Old Rugged

Cross." It was my favorite hymn. I couldn't stop myself from going forward, no more than I could hold back the sun, and I didn't want to. I handed Tudy to Aunt Lottie. Reverend Williams prayed with us, and when I made my way back to the pew, I felt the mirror I was looking into was pure and clean.

When I got home I told the boys all about it and about the preacher's message. They all said, "We want to believe in Jesus, too."

It was set. We were all to be baptized the next Sunday at the Spillway in the North Platte River, all except Lee. I really thought he was too young to know what he was doing. All he talked about was that we were going to get dunked by a minister; so I knew he was not ready.

The pastor explained to the children about Jesus the Savior, and about trusting their lives to Him in sickness and in health, in the bad times and the good. "You tell Him you'll love Him forever and He'll tell you that He'll never go away. He'll be your best Friend and you can talk to Him just like I'm talking to you now. You can ask Him things and He'll help you feel happy inside, way down where even your problems can't reach."

After that little talk I posted a poem Elsie had sent right on my bedroom wall. It stayed there through all the children's growing-up years and is still there today.

Rules for Today

Do nothing that you
Would not like to be doing
When Jesus comes.

Go to no place where you
Would not like to be found
When Jesus comes.

Say nothing that you
Would not like to be saying
When Jesus comes.

I enjoyed the rest of the summer. My misery was gone. I felt kind and loving and giving. I remember rocking the kids to sleep, reading them books and telling them nursery rhymes and crying for joy. Little Lee would ask, "Why are you crying, Mommy?"

"Because I'm so happy," I'd say. *It's like a honeymoon,* I was thinking—*I feel all starry-eyed and knee-deep in roses.*

On July 4 we made ice cream. The kids went to the icehouse to haul some home. During the winter Carlson, the icehouse owner, cut big slabs of ice from the lake, hauled them on sleds and packed them in between layers of straw. It kept the ice good all summer. We'd go over there for ice for lemonade, too.

Porter was one of the heaviest contributors to the Chautauquas. He said a town needed to have "culture." But besides "culture," like politics and sermons, the Chautauquas had singers and musicians, all dressed up. Sometimes people who had been around the world talked about India or China. I still wanted to go traveling. So when we'd get home I'd unroll the big map Nanny Allen had given me so long ago and smooth its crinkled edges and look up the places.

The Chautauqua had a track meet and games in the morning for the kids. I reckon this was when Enie got interested in running. I had always said he had to be fast to get away from Clint and Milt. In the afternoons there'd be plays, "Uncle Tom's Cabin" and the like, and the lectures at night. When they were all through, they'd pack up and move on to the next town.

I thought a good end to the summer would be the Epworth Methodist Institute at Chadron. Besides being fun, it would give us a chance to learn more about the Good Book. It was also a time to relax before moving into the house. I was disappointed that Porter couldn't be with us the whole time. He said he'd drive us down and come get us. I knew he had some deal going, but he wouldn't talk yet. With Porter you had to wait till he was ready to tell you.

When we arrived, we filled our bedticks with straw and took them into big tents where we were to sleep. The boys liked this because they thought they were camping out. In the morning there would be lessons and in the afternoon hikes and games and swimming. It took me several days before I prayed aloud in the prayer circle, like the rest of them. I learned a lot there and made some good friends, but the time I enjoyed most was private devotions. A little house had been built way up high on a hill in the midst of the trees. You couldn't really see it from the road at all. Being all alone there, it seemed like God was all around, whispering through the trees, smiling through the sun. The words in my Bible seemed to jump out at me and I began to understand. It was the most excitement I'd ever felt.

When we got home I tried to share my discoveries with Porter, but it seemed he was so full of house plans and business ideas that he didn't have room for anything else. *Funny,* I thought, *this believing should bring us closer.* In some ways it did because I tried to be more loving to him, but in most ways, we were moving separately, like the two waters at the spillway. It was good to be busy and not to dwell on our problems and the moving in and all we were doing.

In September we had everything boxed and ready to move. On one of the busiest packing days, Enie and Lee began begging for sugar cookies, they both had a sweet tooth. I couldn't resist the looks on their little faces; so there I was, baking in the midst of chaos. Their smiles were so broad as they ate the warm cookies and licked each finger, that I figured it was worth it.

The next day, September 20, I walked in, never to move out again. I held Tudy in my arms. The house had a gabled roof with an upside-down V. I walked up the cement steps to the front porch. On the floor was the biggest Oriental rug I'd ever seen. I counted the bedrooms—one, two, three, four, five. I looked out the window at the side porch. There was a wooden swing. In the big kitchen was a glass cookie jar filled with the rest of my sugar cookies. Enie must have brought them over. I looked down at Tudy. She was all wrapped up. There was a chill in the air. So this was my dream. Did Porter remember and make it come true, or did it just happen? I asked Porter, but he just smiled and asked, "What dream?"

CHAPTER 21

Fall, 1917

In between packing and receiving new furniture, I was mainly thinking about two things. The first was how my dreams had become reality—like when I "saw" Porter before I met him and then the house. The second thing was a prayer that was always on my lips, "Make me pure inside." I had another reason for wanting to be pure other than that I knew God wanted me to be—I saw in the Bible that purity was connected with light. "If, therefore, thine eye be healthy, thy whole body shall be full of light," Jesus said in Matthew 6:22. So I thought that being purer would rid me of my fears of being alone in the dark. I believed that the light which came with purity would drive the darkness right out of me. It seemed to work. The closet nightmare didn't come anymore.

I heard Reverend Bryant give a sermon about

names—how Sarah, Abraham's wife, used to spell her name with an ''i,'' which meant ''quarrelsome,'' but that God, after she believed, changed her name to end in ''h,'' which meant ''princess.'' There were a lot more examples but his point was that names are very important and no accident or chance. I asked him afterwards if there was a way of finding out what your name meant. He said he had a book that he and his wife had used to look up names for their children. He noticed I was excited and said he'd bring it by on Friday.

''Friday?''

I must have looked downcast because then he said, ''Well, what about tomorrow?''

''That would be fine,'' I beamed.

I tried to be polite when he came, offering him coffee and cake before I reached for the book.

''You can keep the book till next Sunday, Inie,'' he said.

His was the longest visit ever. I didn't rush to the book when he left because I wanted to wait till night when the children were asleep and I could be alone. Porter wouldn't be around either.

After the move, he had told me about the business deals he was working on. He was going to sell cars in the winter and head road construction gangs in the summer. So tonight he was off in Lincoln to bid on a construction project for next summer. I wasn't pleased about Porter's being gone most of the summer, but I was glad he was so ambitious. Surely he didn't think that I could go with him. I had five kids now instead of two, and some of them were in school. Porter's plan distressed me, but I tried to avoid words about it.

Turning on the side porch light, I sat down in the swing to look up *Ina Sibyl. Ina,* according to the book, was a form of *Inez,* which meant "purity." A warming went through me like a hot bath on the inside. God had seen to it that my name fit what I was to be! ("There are no accidents with the Good Man," Ma always said.) Finding God was finding what I was born for—not to get married, have babies, or even get rich, but to be one with God and pure like him. My fears of darkness were what the Bad Man wanted for my life. I leafed through the book till I came to *Sibyl. Sibyl* meant "prophetess." *Prophesy,* let's see, didn't that mean being able to foretell the future? Yes, I was sure of it. So that's the reason why I had known what Porter looked like before I saw him, and why I had dreamed about the house and Tudy.

I wondered, *Will I be seeing ahead all my life?* I wasn't sure I wanted to, but then if this was a gift God had for me, I'd see how I could use it for Him. I don't know how long I sat out there rocking back and forth on the swing, reviewing life, thinking about the future, and mulling everything over.

A breeze came up and blew the last of the cotton from the cottonwood trees all over my navy dress. All I wore were dark colors now that I had turned thirty. I had bought the prettiest pink material about two years ago, but I never had gotten to it since we moved off the homestead and got so busy. I'd be making Tudy a dress out of it now. No respectable lady wore bright colors after thirty. It would've depressed me before, but now it didn't matter what I wore. Brushing off the white cotton, I got up to sleep alone—but I was not to be really alone ever again.

I always heard the boys' prayers at night. Lee said, "Now I lay me down to sleep" and added some "God-blesses" on the end. The other boys just talked to God except for Milt who was quiet anyway. He'd pray only if he and I were all alone—not in front of the other boys. Clint was asking the Good Man for a cornet; Milt wanted a sax; Enie, a pony, and Lee, a Charlie Chaplin doll.

This fall, for the first time in my life, I wasn't involved in harvesting. My days were filled with new furniture. Going from a two-room house to an eight-room meant a lot more things had to be bought. The buffet was so large that we had to have Uncle Ide build it in the house. This was all right with me because Aunt Lottie could come visit and rock Tudy while he worked.

Porter got two wicker chairs especially for Ma and me to sit in when she came. Ma's visit was an important one. I had a question to ask her.

"When people die, Ma, do you think they go right to heaven or do they lie in the ground awhile first?" I shuddered even as I heard the words come out of my mouth.

"They go right to heaven, Inie. I know because of what happened to your Grandma Martin—your pa's natural mother. Oh, you wouldn't remember this because you were just three at the time. I was there, though. Pa was, too, and Grandpa Martin, of course.

198

He had told us all to come because he reckoned this would be Grandma's final hour. She was lying there so peaceful with her eyes closed, but she was still breathing. All of a sudden, she sat straight up and held out her arms crying, 'Jesus, Jesus. They've come for me! See the angels and the chariot?' Then she fell back. Grandpa checked her pulse. She was gone, but none of us doubted where she had gone."

Ma's story had taken away my fear of death, but I still wondered about being buried alive, and I still felt the need to discuss it with somebody.

The cold weather came early and I was glad. It meant Christmas was coming, and Christmas in our new house was going to be something special. I was thankful the lake had frozen over because the boys could go skating, and Milt could trap muskrats and sell the hides. I was glad Milt was busy and out of the house. I only had one blind left with a roller in it; he had used all the others to make parts for his little airplanes.

One sure sign Christmas was coming soon was Grandpa Baker's sackful of black walnuts. He sent it all the way from Salem inside a big barrel. When I saw Porter lugging that in, I could almost taste black walnut cake. We also ordered salted peanuts, sugar candy, gingersnaps, and marshmallow creams from the Sears catalog. These would all be a surprise laid out on our big round table in the living room in big boxes and a five-gallon wooden candy bucket next to our tree. The children would be delighted. Porter promised a real tree all the way from Colorado. "If I have to go there and cut it myself," he joked. None of those dead branches wrapped in colored paper for us!

The children helped me make taffy. It gave them something to do while waiting for Santa to come. Of course, only Lee and Tudy believed in him still, but the elder boys sure believed in the presents they were going to get. We'd pull that taffy until it was porous and white like smooth satin. I kept the boys busy in the afternoon, delivering popcorn balls to our friends and neighbors. Then right before church they hung up their stockings.

We were going to pick up Porter on the late afternoon train and then go right to church. He had gone to Lincoln again to bid on a road construction job. I wanted to protest, but I kept silent. I longed for the early days and for the homestead days when we worked side by side. I had thought then, the more money we had, the more time we'd have for each other, but it didn't work out that way. I had grown into my own world of tending for the new house and the children.

Porter, elated over his wealth from the invention, was in the world of making money—setting up a car business for the winter, and road construction work for the summer. Our worlds didn't cross much any more. Lying silently next to him, I'd think of when I had held his head after Milt was born and he had cried and cried as he told me about Tibby. How close we had been then! Would we ever be that close again? Did Porter feel the lack of it as I did? He gave no indication of his feelings even when he kissed or touched me. He always tried to be so jolly. But I wondered if he was really happy.

These were my thoughts as we drove in to get Porter, all of us in our Sunday best. I hardly ever drove, except if it was less than a mile. Seemed I'd scare the boys out of their wits. I laugh now as I thought of their screaming, "Stay between the fences, Ma! Watch out for that cow! Oh-wee! Close your eyes, everyone!" People were already getting off the train when we drove up. I hoped we hadn't missed greeting him. I watched family after family kiss and hug, their arms full of presents. It was a wonderful sight. But no Porter. I asked the conductor if everyone had gotten off. "Yes, madam," he said.

Thinking he had missed the train closing his business deal, I went to the ticket office and asked, "When's the next train due in?"

"This is the last one tonight."

"How about tomorrow?"

"We don't run on Christmas, ma'am."

Now, what was I to do? How could we celebrate without Porter? This was such a special Christmas, too, and today was Tudy's first birthday. I stood there watching the train pull out slowly, wiping the tears away with the back of my white glove. I had sewed little Christmas trees on them just for tonight. *The children*. The thought of them helped me collect my scattered wits. *I must be cheerful for the children*. But the thought of putting out the presents and filling the stockings alone made my insides ache.

"Pa wasn't on the train," I said as I started the car.

"In church we'll say a prayer for his safety." The children didn't say a word. With the hum of the engine and the mention of church, a new idea entered my head. *God is my Friend.* I said the words slowly. This new relationship was getting closer every day. From a honeymoon of overflowing happiness, God and I had settled into living every day with each other. A quiet joy was with me in everything I did. Even now, though I was close to tears, the joy was there.

The service was the most meaningful ever. Before, I'd enjoyed the carols and candlelight because of the pleasant memories they brought back, but now I listened to the words,

"Joy to the world, the Lord is come."

Yes, the Lord had come to me. To *me,* Inie, a little nobody living out in a small town in western Nebraska, the Lord of all creation had come!

A light snow was falling so we stepped outside. I hugged each of the boys. I decided that part of our Christmas festivities would include reading the Christmas story and talking about it.

After Tudy blew out her candle, with help from Lee, and I heard everybody's prayers, I set about to decorate the tree. I decided to include Clint who seemed happy to be considered grown-up enough to surprise the little ones. We clipped on candles and hung strings of popcorn and cranberries. We laid out the cake for Santa Claus with a glass of milk. We hung letters from the posts in the living room. On the round table we put the cookies, candies, and peanuts. In the stockings were apples from Fall City and even grapefruit.

When it came time to set out the presents, I sent Clint to bed. Then out from under my bed I took a cornet for Clint, a sax for Milt, a mandolin for Enie, and Lee's Charlie Chaplin doll. Tudy had a lot of little toys and a doll, of course. I took out my present for Porter too and the ache returned. I left the light on that night as I slept. The old closet nightmare threatened. I decided that if I gave into pity and sadness too much, my old fears would haunt me again.

I couldn't get back to sleep. Maybe it wasn't all Porter's fault that he acted the way he did—sometimes taking off on his own pursuits. Maybe he'd been spoiled. If he was, I could understand it. After losing two boys, his ma and pa were so glad to have him, it would've been hard not to give him everything he wanted. I remembered the big house in Salem and Porter's name on his bedroom door. He was raised with money all right—he and his three sisters.

My mind was spinning. I thought of Sam Hall. Now to say I hadn't thought of him in years would be wrong. I thought of him especially when Porter was gone or when I felt distant from him. But this Christmas I had a special reason for thinking of Sam. I'd received some postcards from him. The first two cards were unsigned. They had bouquets of flowers on them with these verses:

In pleasure's dream, or
    sorrow's hour,
In crowded hall or lonely
    bower,
The business of my soul

shall be
Forever to remember thee.

'Tis said that absence conquers love,
    But, oh! believe it not;
I've tried, alas! its power to prove,
    But thou art not forgot.

On the back of one was written "Hello, *au revoir.*"
On the back of another was "Dearest, in memory's
golden chain, drop one link for me." The third card
read the words from a hymn;

For you I am praying,
for you I am praying,
for you I am praying,
I am praying for you.

and was signed "SJH." On the front of this card was
a man leaning over a fence to hold a lady's hand
saying, "When I whisper I love you so, won't you say
you love me, too?" The fourth card showed a lady
peering over a garden wall at a dreamy-eyed suitor.
From her face to his was a beam of sunshine. The card
read "We'll be wedded to each other and the sunshine
will smile on us, too."

Was Sam out of his head? I was already married. I
decided that he was just dreaming about what might
have been. This card said on the back, "Sweetheart,
sweetheart, in your eyes love beams, hope of my
hope, dream of my dreams, my sweetheart." The fifth
card had writing from front to back.

Only to follow you, Dearest, only to find you,
Only to feel for one instant the touch of your hand,

Only to tell you once of the love you left behind you;
to tell you the world without you is like a desert of
    sand,
That the flowers have lost their perfume, the rose its
    splendor
And the scenes of nature seem lost in a dull eclipse.
That joy went out with the glance of your eyes so
    tender
And beauty passed with the lovely smile on your lips. I
never dreamed it was you who kindled the morning
Or folded the evening purple in peace so sweet
But you took the whole world's rapture without a
    warning.
And left me naught save the print of your patient feet.
I count the days and hours that hold us asunder
And long for death's friendly hand that shall rend in
    twain
With the glorious lightning flash and the golden
    thunder.
Ye clouds of earth and give me my own again.

This poem left me breathless. Did Sam still love me
this much? It made me feel sad, heavy with sadness.
Thinking about Sam and Oklahoma brought back a
flood of memories. Sabrina, berry-picking, school,
Uncle Jim's stories, Indians, play parties, and Dick.
My mind was so full of memories that I prayed,
*"God, use these thoughts, and help me to thank You
for each of them."* I thought about my choices in the
past—had they been right? I decided then I must never
regret. Anyway, regretting must be a sin because you
couldn't change the past and it only filled you with
sadness. God would have to use my mistakes and my
past just the way it was. I reckon I fell asleep praying.

Ma always said, "If you can't sleep, pray. The Devil would rather have you sleep than pray. It works every time."

I woke up sad and empty but then remembered, *Christmas morning! The children will be so excited!* I heard the church bell ring as usual.

The littlest ones got to go in first and look in their stockings so Tudy toddled in, falling a few times, and turned her stocking upside down. The boys laughed at her, calling the apple a ball and trying to bounce it. Then Lee came in, next Enie, then Milt, then Clint. We all opened our presents together. In the middle of our opening there was a knock on the door. *Porter,* I thought and then dismissed it. Porter wouldn't knock. A strange man was there. I was frightened. "Has something happened to Porter?"

"Ma'am, Porter gave me some money to deliver this." He brought in a big box. The children were all excited. It was a sewing machine—the fanciest one I'd ever seen. I was so happy I kept running my hand over its gold letters: "Singer."

The boys and Tudy were happy with their presents, saying, "It's just what we prayed for." Enie liked his, too, but he kept glancing outside.

Porter came about an hour later. I didn't hear him over the noise of all the boys practicing their instruments—and noise it was, not music at all, yet. He put his hands over my eyes, "Guess who?" I thought it was Clintie who had sneaked up behind me but, no, he was over there making horrible honks on his cornet.

"Porter!" I turned around, kissing his hands as I held on to them.

"Say, you glad to see me? I tried calling, but all the lines were busy. I sure hated to miss Christmas. I got a man for a high price to drive me here."

"The machine, Porter, it's beautiful."

"I thought you'd like it."

"Come here, Enie." Porter led him toward the window. "Oh, Papa" he cried, and he bounded out the door. The other boys followed. A pony with a new saddle was tied to our tree.

I didn't ask Porter why he hadn't made it home, and he didn't volunteer any reasons. We were silent, facing each other. I thought of Porter all alone in his hotel room Christmas Eve. Here I had been thinking of myself alone, when I had the joy of the children with me. I gave Porter my present—a jeweled gold watch.

Porter was home, and he was looking at me the way he had before we were married. I was about to look away when, instead, I reached up and put my arms around him.

As he bent down to kiss me, I thought, *Now Christmas has come*.

MEET THE AUTHOR

KAREN BAKER KLETZING lives in Vina Del Mar, Chile, where she and her husband, David, serve with the South American Mission Society of the Episcopal Church. Karen is a graduate of Wheaton College, where she majored in literature and from Indiana University from which she holds a doctorate in reading education. She has taught at the high school and college levels and served with her husband as parish co-director of Christian education. The Kletzings have two children, Juliette, 5, and Davy, 3.

The story of *Ina* is based on the life of Ina Baker, Karen's grandmother, who was a pioneer and homesteader in Oklahoma and Nebraska panhandle around the turn of the century. Research for the book began with Karen's desire for her children to know their grandmother and to benefit from her life.

A Letter To Our Readers

Dear Reader:

Pioneering is an exhilarating experience, filled with opportunities for exploring new frontiers. The Zondervan Corporation is proud to be the first major publisher to launch a series of inspirational romances designed to inspire and uplift as well as to provide wholesome entertainment. In order that we might better contribute to your reading enjoyment, we would appreciate your taking a few minutes to respond to the following questions and return to:

Anne Severance, Editor
Serenade/Saga Books
749 Templeton Drive
Nashville, Tennessee   37205

1. Did you enjoy reading INA?

  ☐ Very much. I would like to see more books by this author!
  ☐ Moderately
  ☐ I would have enjoyed it more if _____

2. Where did you purchase this book? _____

3. What influenced your decision to purchase this book?

  ☐ Cover   ☐ Back cover copy
  ☐ Title   ☐ Friends
  ☐ Publicity   ☐ Other _____

4. Please rate the following elements (from 1 to 10):

☐ heroine   ☐ Plot
☐ Hero   ☐ Inspirational theme
☐ Setting   ☐ Secondary characters

5. Which settings do you prefer?

_____   _____

_____   _____

6. What are some inspirational themes you would like to see treated in future Serenade books?

_____   _____

_____   _____

7. Would you be interested in reading other Serenade/ Serenata or Serenade/Saga Books?

☐ Very interested
☐ Moderately interested
☐ Not interested

8. Please indicate your age range:

☐ Under 18   ☐ 25–34   ☐ 46–55
☐ 18–24   ☐ 35–45   ☐ Over 55

9. Would you be interested in a Serenade book club? If so, please give us your name and address:

Name _____

Occupation _____

Address _____

City _____ State _____ Zip _____